Tzu Kingdom

The Santa Paws Trilogy

Karen Chilvers & Gill Eastgate

Illustrated by Michelle Smith

Front cover design by Wendy Simko

Published by New Generation Publishing in 2019

First Edition

ISBN 978-1-78955-712-1

www.newgeneration-publishing.com

New Generation Publishing

Queen Coffee's Prologue

About six hundred dog years ago, Shih Tzus only lived in one land. It was in the Far, Far East and they had lived, played and cuddled there for thousands of dog years before that.

It was a beautiful summer day and they were so happy skipping, jumping and chasing each other about in their palace grounds.

All of a sudden, from absolutely nowhere, a freak storm began. The sun went into hiding and gave way to intense windy rain, black clouds, thunder and lightning.

It caught the tzus unaware and they ran for cover and waited for the storm to pass.

The storm stopped as suddenly as it had begun and the gang ventured out of their hiding place – the adult tzus first for safety, ushering the youngsters out when they knew it was safe.

Even though the sturdy tzus were unscathed by the storm, some more delicate creatures were not so fortunate.

As they gathered up their toys, one of the youngest tzus, Leo, heard a faint cry of help. It was coming from the lake. They had never ventured so far before, but now, someone clearly needed their help.

They ran down the grassy slopes as fast as their little legs could go and found fairies of all colours caught in an enormous fishing net, tired, upset and exhausted.

They too had been taken by surprise, blown off course by the winds and were now trapped with their intricate wings, and their very lives, in serious peril.

Without even thinking, Leo divided the tzus in to action teams and they all set to work with their nimble paws and delicate teeth, working in pairs to unhook every fairy and his or her tiny wings. The complicated rescue was eventually completed with all fairies free, unhurt and fluttering once again. It had taken hours, in to the night, but the tzus and their teamwork, patience and skill had saved the fairies from perishing.

Leo and his friends wished the fairies well and went back to the palace, pleased to be able to help and proud of how they had all worked together.

The next day, he was surprised to see a small delegation of fairies appear at the gates of their home. They thanked the tzus once again for saving them from such mortal danger and asked if there was anything they could gift to them. The tzus turned to Leo – after all it had been his long ears that had heard their cries for help.

Leo could only think of one thing after his adventure to the lake...to see the world.

The fairies then decreed that all Shih Tzus could use their fairy door network to visit new lands...shrinking down to squeeze through with fairy magic.

After this, Shih Tzus started to spread out through the world, making new friends and settling in new lands. Nonetheless they missed snuggling up, eating and playing games with each other and soon wished they had somewhere to meet up and this time, they asked the fairies for their help.

The fairies understood and set about setting up a palace within the fairy kingdom where the tzus could meet. They called it Tzu Kingdom on the condition that they would keep it beautiful, they would keep it secret and that they would elect the wisest tzu to be their King or Queen and they would see that it was always used for good.

The tzus accepted this offer and were quick to make Leo their first King for his bravery and leadership qualities.

Over the next few years, Leo made Tzu Kingdom what it is today and laid down the foundations for all future Kings and Queens to keep the promise they made to the fairies...

The Santa Paws

One sunny, bright afternoon on a sparkling beach on the shores of the Atlantic Ocean, an enchanted Lady shares an ice cream with her soft coated wheaten terrier.

He looks up at her with his loving eyes, thanking her as he does each day for giving him a loving home and appreciating her kindness to him and others. To say he landed on his paws the day he found her is an understatement.

She gives him another scoop and tells him she was lucky to find him, with a glowing smile and a happy tear.

As often is the way with rescue dogs and their owners as they face life's ups and downs, after a while they cannot remember who saved whom.

He so wished he could tell her his big secret, but he took an oath to keep it although, sometimes he thinks she might suspect his role in the dog world.

For Seamus – Shay – is Santa Paws.

Santa Paws Land & Tzu Kingdom

The friendship between the two dog worlds extends back generations, long before Santa Paws Shay or King Bailey and Queen Coffee. However, it's rumoured that the current Santa Paws has a particular soft spot for the shih tzu world and often takes up the opportunity to share some Tzu Bakery delicacies with his dear friends.

Shay believes, quite firmly, that the Christmas spirit should be shared all year round and knows that love, friendship and kind deeds are the very ethos of Tzu Kingdom.

It is no surprise that a photo of him with his pals 'King B' and 'Queen C' adorns the Royal Quarters.

And perhaps, just perhaps, there was a good reason why this was where his sleigh crash landed one festive season.

"It is as it is, as it was and as it always will be," as King Bailey says...

Tzu Kingdom
Santa Bailey

★ ★ ★ ★ ★ ★ ★

Chapter 1

Paddy Boo the Shih Tzu jumped through the fairy doors hardly able to contain his excitement. It was Christmas Eve. The party of the year, hosted by King Bailey and Queen Coffee, the rulers of Tzu Kingdom, was on tonight. He already knew it was going to be a blast!

He let out an enormous burp (as all tzus did after leaping through the fairy doors.) He landed in the Welcome Room and skidded across the floor to the desk. If there was one thing you could say about Paddy, he knew how to make an entrance.

"Evening ladies," he said to Carmen, Suki and Zena, the welcomer tzus on duty. The ladies were handing out jingle bells to everyone who arrived at the party to add to their front paws and tails.

"Evening Paddy," said the elder ladies, laughing at Paddy's infectious enthusiasm. He loved Tzu Kingdom and this was his favourite night of the year for sure.

"No Mitch then?" said Carmen, sounding a little disappointed.

"Oh, erm, no, no," said Paddy, equally disheartened.

Paddy had so wanted Mitch to come with him for the Christmas party. He had achieved so much in Tzu Kingdom as a scout - he wanted to show his new big brother what he had done in Scout Tower, how he had kept the Tzu Promise to the fairies to use the Kingdom for good. This promise they had made in exchange for a wonderful kingdom where tzus could party and enjoy each other's company. But just like every time this past year, since they had joined as one family in Belfast, he had made an excuse.

"Is Stan here?" enquired Paddy, deliberately changing the subject before he got too upset at being snubbed. Again.

"Yes Paddy, he's at the bar talking to Colin".

"Catch you all later for a Christmas hug!" he shouted as he sprinted in to the Party Room.

Chapter 2

Stanley was leaning over the bar deciding on what flavour milkshake he wanted, when all of a sudden a pair of paws dug in his ribs. He jumped and giggled, being very ticklish.

"Surprise!" said a loud bark and he spun around. "Paddy!" he said, high pawing his best friend and getting a tickle in his tummy for his trouble.

"You always get caught out, when will you learn?" said their good friend Colin, with laughing eyes.

The boys all clinked milkshakes and Stanley looked over Paddy's shoulder.

"Is Mitch on his way?" he said.

"He's not coming," said Paddy and, before Stanley or Colin could respond he got very defensive indeed.

"Well, he's a busy tzu. I mean he *wanted* to come but he had to help Dada down in the shed making sure the human boys' toys work tomorrow...I mean imagine if they open up their gifts from Santa tomorrow and they can't get them to work it'll be pandemonium with crying and upset and no one will want dinner and I won't get me plate of turkey n sausages and it will all end in tears, me mam will be all "can't we just have a nice family day without a hoo hah and a fuss..."...it's a big responsibility being a brother to his own human and my human and me you know and Mitchy, well, he takes it seriously, and he's the mechanic in the family and Dada can't get everything ready without his assistant passing him up hammers and bolts and boy stuff and, well, he can't just drop everything and come partying willy nilly whenever he feels like it and leave his responsibilities behind - well can he - and beside that he still gets them big burps when he comes through the fairy doors – you know he suffers with his wind..." he garbled all in one breath.

"OK Pads," said Colin whilst Stanley just pulled a startled face, "calm down".

"I only asked..." said Stanley to no-one in particular, wondering how they could get back on a more jovial platform. Things had got quite serious all of a sudden.

At that very point, some of the girls arrived in their Christmas best, looking an absolute delight.

Maisie, Nancy, Phoebe, Kiki, Alice and Lola swept in to the party room looking sparkly - laughing and dancing across the floor.

'Wow,' thought the boys, those girls know how to swish!

Chapter 3

Maisie had no idea why the boys were looking glum when they had been so looking forward to the Christmas party, but she wasn't going to get involved. Fun needed to be had – now!

She jumped over the bar, put her paws on her hips and ordered the bar keep tzus to provide 'party paraphernalia'. All the tzus loved Maisie and her ability to take control of the situation. In under a minute, all the drinks had little paper umbrellas, cocktail sticks spiked with fruit and multi-coloured sparklers.

The party had finally begun!

"Come on," said Maisie, "let's go and listen to the band".

'Tzu Aroo' had just taken to the stage and the young tzus were delighted to be able to get right up to the front. On account of his bad leg, Colin had stayed behind chatting to his bar-keep friends and welcoming any new tzus for whom this was their first Kingdom party. Colin, despite being young, worked as a Welcomer. Although it was officially his night off, he never considered himself to be really off-duty. He was always there to extend a paw to the new friends that the scouts brought through the fairy doors. Nancy, an elder tzu, had gone to find her friend Queen Coffee.

"*Tzu Aroo* is the best band*,"* sighed Maisie. She had managed to catch them rehearsing most days this past week. They swayed as the musicians played soft music as more and more fluffy coated tzus arrived in the Party Room. The hubbub was getting louder and the music played a little louder too, making them tingle with anticipation of the dancing, food and partying ahead.

"King Bailey and Queen Coffee will be here soon," said Phoebe looking over towards the door to the Royal Chamber.

"Do you think there'll be a Paw Stomp tonight?" asked Stanley, hoping that there was so he could dance with his besties.

"There'll be a special one for Christmas tonight Stan," said Lola, "that's what the bells are for!" She jangled her front paws and wiggled her tail as a demonstration.

"It's as much about the jingles as the stomping tonight!" jingled Kiki, shaking everything that shook.

"Hello Tzus, how y'all doing?" said a husky American voice over the microphone.

Stanley and Paddy felt their jaws drop at the sophisticated sight before them on stage and used their paws to put them back in position, much to the girls' amusement. Holding the microphone and in the spotlight was a female figure with long, wavy black and silver curly fur, glamorously glorious ears and a furry leg peeping out from long red dress. She suddenly appeared like a mirage, mesmerising every fur in the room.

Tuxie was in town.

Chapter 4

Tuxie got the party started with an energetic rendition of *'There's No Pawty Like a Tzu Club Pawty'* and followed it up with a rocking version of *'Who Let the Tzus Out?'* with lots of audience participation.

Kiki and Lola always knew the latest dance moves. They took up position at the front and hopped, swirled and jumped through the routines. As senior rescuers, they were very fit. To her delight, little Maisie, who had grabbed Alice to be her partner, matched them pawstep-for-pawstep. Paddy and Stanley were puffed out by the end.

"You boys had better have a drink and a sit down with Colin before the **Jingle Paw Stomp**," she said, once again with her paws on her hips.

But there was a reprieve anyway as Phoebe, who was a very tall tzu, jumped up excitedly.

"Look, look, it's Bailey and Coffee - they are coming up on to the stage! Oh, that's unusual?"

King Bailey and Queen Coffee were loved by all the tzus in the Kingdom. There was an enormous round of applause as they climbed on to the stage, paw-in-paw. There had been lots of ups and downs this year but they had come through the Kingdom stronger for their leadership and love.

Tuxie was ever so surprised to see the royal couple on stage with the band and she offered King Bailey the microphone.

"Give us a song!" shouted Nancy from the bar, to everyone's amusement.

Bailey laughed, "Me sing? That's the last thing we want...I don't want to ruin the evening!" he chuckled and then cleared his throat.

"As many of you know, this is Tuxie and Kemp's last night as members of Tzu Aroo....no don't be sad..." he said, as a big 'aww' went up in the Party Room.

"Kemp joined just a couple of years ago on bass guitar when dear young Flash closed his eyes for the last time but Tuxie, along with Lennon, was one of the founder members some considerable dog years ago. Well, the time comes when the old guard has to take a back seat and, although I am sure she will be tempted back as a guest turn, Tuxie is going to retire to the sunshine coast with Kemp and their human family. We will still see them regularly, but they won't be able to take part in the band's hectic rehearsal schedule and are going to enjoy a slower pace of life".

"So," said Queen Coffee, "we just have a couple of small tokens of appreciation for you both".

She presented Kemp with a bottle of vintage Tzu Kingdom Marrowbone Sauce and then produced a box for Tuxie to open. She gasped as she opened it and then held a beautiful sparkling necklace to the crowd.

"SPEECH, SPEECH," came the cry.

"Well you wonderful furs. This is a just an amazing surprise. Thank you Bailey and Coffee, you indeed rule this place with great love, you teach us lion-dogs to be as brave as lions and we learn so much from you every day.

"Thank you to the rest of the band for their support – we are a team and it will continue as, of course, Kemp and I will be involved in the auditions that begin in the New Year.

"We love all our friends, near and far, with us tonight and, well, elsewhere. Please raise a glass...to Tzu Kingdom!"

"TZU KINGDOM!" came the response.

"Just one more thing Tuxie," said Queen Coffee, "will you lead us in the Jingle Paw Stomp?"

Chapter 5

The special Christmas 'Jingle Paw Stomp' was so fast and funny that there were giggling tzus in piles all over the floor. As well as stomping with their boots, they were jingling their bells throughout, even once they had finally fallen over due to the sheer speed of the dance.

Kiki and Lola were the last two dancing as the Stomp finished with an enormous crash. Maisie and Alice got a special round of applause for almost getting to the end!

"Wow...that really was loud," said Colin, from his bar stool.

"It was too loud," said Nancy, her ears pricked up. "It sounded like an explosion to me".

The room fell quiet so the sound of thundering paws made every tzu prick up their ears as Carmen ran in from the Welcome Room.

"Mayday Mayday," she gasped, "Bonnie just called down from Scout Tower...it's Santa Paws. He's crashed at high speed in the Tzu Kingdom garden and he's hurt – badly hurt".

Chapter 6

The Tzu Kingdom garden was strewn with presents and a variety of dogs. Some were sitting up holding their heads in their paws and some were wandering around the garden in a daze.

In the midst of the chaos was a large sleigh and, poking out from underneath were two very long, but alarmingly still, Soft Coated Wheaten Terrier legs.

"Shay...erm...I mean...Santa Paws," shouted Bailey, his short little legs speeding up as he ran closer to the sleigh. When he got to the scene he tried with all his might to lift it off but he was so small it was just far too heavy. From all around tzus joined him, and with a mighty 'One...Two...Three' they all pushed and heaved and upturned the sleigh away from its injured prisoner.

For a minute everything was silent as the red and white cloaked figure remained motionless. The King moved closer whilst every fur watched in anticipation wondering if, and hoping that, everything was going to be OK.

"Santa Paws?" Bailey whispered as he moved in close and stroked the soft coat of the motionless dog.

"King B? Is that you?" said a deep voice and one eye opened and looked at his old friend. Coffee appeared by their side, with a glass of water and a blanket.

"Is this what a fellow has to do to get a drink in your kingdom?" laughed Santa Paws.

"Seamus, you always did know how to make an entrance!" laughed Coffee.

She passed him the water and checked him all over. He was certainly hurt, even if only cuts and bruises. He was definitely concussed so they had to get him inside to the Comforter Wing to be looked after. King Bailey summoned Paddy, Stanley, Tanner and Lennon over to carry him through and, taking a leg each, they squeezed him through the patio doors and into the Comforter Wing where he was made comfortable on several bean bags.

Chapter 7

The younger tzus gathered in the kitchen whilst the elders tended to Santa Paws.

"Why do Bailey and Coffee call him 'Shay-mouse'" said a confused Maisie.

"I suspect that's his real name, you know what his humans gave to him. It's an Irish name with a funny spelling for how it's said! I know a few Seamuses back in Belfast," said Paddy, sagely, "and one big humpy grumpy Mitch too!"

"Why isn't he here tonight Pads?" asked Stanley, still curious and risking another strop from his friend, but he had to know.

Paddy sighed and finally began to explain why he had been in such a bad mood earlier.

"I really don't know Stan because he made a paw promise – yes – a paw promise. I think he does it to annoy me and make me look stupid. He's always winding me up – he pinches me toys, he pinches me food AND he pinches me mam for a lap cuddle too, and that is most certainly NOT allowed!"

Paddy had been lion brave this past year. His mam, his human brother and he had moved over the sea from Liverpool because his mam had decided that they would go and make a new family with his new dad, a second human brother and Mitch, a tzu much older than Paddy. He had met Mitch before of course, when he went for a holiday to approve his mum's choice of fella. But he was a bit shocked that after last year's Christmas when it was just the three of them and, mostly, him and his mam, as they packed up their things, loaded up the car, put a "To Let" sign outside their house and set sail for

Belfast. He said a sad and emotional goodbye to his friends, his park and his garden but, he pondered, I am getting a tzu brother so it'll always be play time now.

But, although they played occasionally and talked about tzu stuff, Mitch was a little set in his ways. He didn't even come to Tzu Kingdom any more, on account of the terrible wind he experienced when he jumped through the fairy doors. He had paw-promised his little brother he would at least come to the Christmas party. Paddy had been so looking forward to showing him Scout Tower and telling him about his plans for modernising the telescope system. Not to mention his 'taster sessions' - he was going to offer them to the younger tzus who might want to consider being a Scout when they were old enough. He felt let down, and more than a little cross.

"Why does he pinch your mam Paddy when he has his Dada?"

"He hogs them both Stanley, he's a menace. I can't say I am looking forward to Christmas now and I was too, with my new family, but he's ruined it. Ruined it".

***

Back in the Comforter Bedroom, Coffee had put her paw firmly down after examining Shay's injuries. He was generally ok, but terribly dizzy and unsteady on his enormous paws.

Santa Paws would not fly tonight, unless a solution could be found, quickly. As far as the dogs of the world were concerned, Christmas was cancelled.

Chapter 8

Santa Paws – Shay - had argued and argued with Queen Coffee but she wouldn't hear of it – he simply wasn't well enough to fly tonight.

"But imagine the faces of the dogs all over the world Sweet Coffee Cup – they will be by the tree or at the dinner table watching their humans and cats open their presents, yet they will have nothing".

"You won't change my mind by calling me cute names Mr Seamus Soft Coated Wheaten Terrier. I thought you knew me..." she smiled, wryly.

"That really won't work Shay – how many years have you known her?" Bailey laughed.

Nancy, who knew them all so well, had been looking out of the window in the Comforter Wing, admiring the stars in the winter sky. She turned to her friends, stroking her beard with her paw.

"Well, pardon me, but this old dog has been around the park a few times and she might just have a plan".

They all pricked up their ears and turned to face Nancy.

"Shay, do you have any Magic Santa Dust left?"

He nodded.

"Does it work on any breed of dog?"

He nodded again.

"So, we would be looking for a responsible dog of any breed – maybe a tzu, who is wise and able to command respect amongst his team, has a practical paw and heart filled with love?"

He nodded again. "Yes Nancy, all those things as well as the bravery of a lion".

"Well, I think we need look no further do we?" and looked over at the Tzu King.

Bailey jumped. "Are you joking Nancy?"

"No, not at all. I just can't think of anyfur better qualified – after all aren't you the King of Lion Dogs?"

Coffee broke her silence and patter pawed over to her husband and flung her paws around him.

"Oh Bailey please, you have to be Santa Paws...just for one night. I would be so proud of you – we all would – and think of the puppies and their little faces..." she said, excitedly.

Bailey thought and paced for a moment. He was very small, six times smaller than Shay at least and he had no experience of this sort of task. Shay had been Santa for the last seven Christmases, he knew the route, he knew how to fly and he knew where to deliver the presents to. He seemed to sense what the King was worried about.

"King B – you can do it. Don't worry about any of the technical stuff, a sprinkle of magic and you'd be away. We will find you an elf and some sleigh-dogs. You really are the best solution and look, you would make Coffee so proud".

He looked at his Queen, noted her excited anticipation to think that he would not only be her beloved husband and King but also Santa Paws. Looking in her hopeful eyes, he just couldn't resist.

"OK, I'll do it. For one night only, I'm Santa Bailey!"

Chapter 9

Paddy, Stanley and Maisie arrived in the Comforter Room with soup and toast for the injured dogs and weren't expecting the excited scene they saw before them.

"What's going on here?" said Stanley, passing soups to two bandaged labradoodles and a dizzy border terrier.

Nancy explained that Bailey was to be Santa Paws for the night and the youngsters agreed it was a wonderful idea.

"So, how are you going to make Bailey in to Santa?" asked a confused Maisie.

"Well, said Coffee, we will sprinkle some Christmas magic on him and Bailey will turn in to Santa. We will find some volunteers – we need an Organiser Elf and some sleigh dogs – we sprinkle them also and we are OFF!" said the Queen.

"Cool," said Paddy, "will the Christmas magic fix the sleigh too?"

The elder tzus went silent. "Oh dear," a sad Bailey shook his head, "no, it only works on dogs".

Paddy passed his plate of buttery toast to Santa Paws' Organiser Elf, a Pekingese named Binky. "I've got a plan, be right back!" he shouted, as he headed towards the fairy doors.

Stanley knew exactly where he was going but before he could say anything, the door opened again and a vision in red stood sparkling in the doorway.

"Can I help with any fur's treatment?" said Tuxie.

"Wowser...I feel better already!" said Shay, staring at Tuxie, and everyone giggled.

"Oh Shay...you know how to make a mature lady feel good! How about a song?" She settled on the four-poster bed she started to sing, leaning against a post, unaccompanied, to the furs as they ate their toast...

"Have yourself, a furry little Christmas,

let the good food flow...

Wrap yourself in warm clothes

and enjoy the snow..."

Chapter 10

Every fur clapped as Tuxie finished her song. It had cheered everyone up immensely and the colour was coming back to the cheeks of those who had been involved in the crash landing.

"Well," said Queen Coffee, "we must do introductions now everyone is feeling a little better. "Shay, why don't you introduce your team, it will help us to understand whom we need to fill their boots and help our 'Santa Bailey'," - she let out a little giggle.

Santa Paws looked at the young furs and noticed how well behaved they were, knowing this was down to Bailey and Coffee and the way they ruled their Kingdom with such poise, trust and respect. They were a legend, much talked about and revered in dog circles.

Shay introduced 'Team Christmas' and he could see they were mesmerised. He noticed that the littlest tzu there, that Coffee had introduced to him as Maisie, was especially attentive and making notes on a little notebook with a sparkly pink pencil.

Shay's original team for the night consisted of a team of sleigh-dogs. Two terriers - Clapton and Marley – for strength, two long legged dogs – Custard and Marmalade – for speed, and two labradoodles - Teddy and Blondie – for enthusiasm.

In addition, of course, there was Binky, Santa Paws' Elf Dog, who had the list of all the deliveries they had to make on Christmas Eve.

"Are there any on the naughty list this year?" asked Bailey.

"No, Bailey," confirmed Shay, "there are no bad dogs my friend, just bad owners".

They shook their heads, thinking about the dogs who were mistreated and unloved. This got Queen Coffee thinking.

"Shay, are there presents for all the dogs who are in shelters this year, waiting and waiting to go to a new home and praying for a better life?"

"Not many this year sweet Coffee, not nearly as many as there used to be. People have changed; they are not as generous as they once were. Time was when I could give a toy to every home-needing dog but not now. Sad as it is, humans and their children are so worried about which device they will have for a gift that, well, many of them don't even spare a thought for those less fortunate. I think we have a few toys, Binky has been trying to work out who is the worthiest, but it's been difficult...how can you decide a conundrum like that?"

Maisie jumped to her paws.

"We can fix this right here and now," and she stomped her paw in a fashion that made her big sister, Nancy, brim with pride.

"How?" said Stanley, getting out of his comfy beanbag, supportively.

"Well, it seems to me that we are all very lucky dogs and that we have loads of toys and blankets that, come tomorrow morning, if what Santa Paws says is true, we will have more of the same. So, by my reckoning, we all have a toy that we are not that fond of or a blanket that we can spare. Therefore, my suggestion my Mr Stanley Shih Tzu is that we all run home, I mean ALL of us, every tzu that is here at the party, we all run home and grab a few things and scamper back here..."

"...and hopefully by the time we are back Paddy will have got Mitch to come through and fix the sleigh too," added Stanley.

It was a brilliant plan and she knew she had impressed the elder tzus.

"There's not a moment to waste!"

She grabbed Stanley's paw and headed back down the corridor with him to the Party Room.

Tuxie jumped off the bed, excitedly, her eyelashes fluttering and trying to catch her breath.

"Mitch? My Mitchy?"

Chapter 11

Mitch was ambling around the garden minding his own business when Paddy jumped through their fairy door and burped loudly. He smiled at the noise he made as he landed on the grass.

Dada was backwards and forwards tidying up after a few last-minute fixes to some Christmas presents.

"MITCH, MITCH are you coming through to Tzu Kingdom now, like you paw promised?"

Mitch was embarrassed; he had no intention of going to the party if truth be known. It would just be too upsetting because he knew Tuxie would be singing tonight. He couldn't bear the thought of listening to her unique rendition of *'Santa Paws is Coming to Town'* knowing that she no longer loved him.

He had managed to put his wonderful Tzu Kingdom out of his mind until Paddy came to live with him, all full of news from Scout Tower and most importantly, about *Tzu Aroo*. Mitch had been their roadie, helping the band set up for their gigs. He helped Tuxie run through her sound check but since Kemp had arrived on the scene things changed. He had thought of her every single day and dreamed about her every single nap and sometimes he thought maybe he imagined what they had.

To Paddy, he had always blamed his non-appearance at Tzu Kingdom on his terrible wind and his new little brother had always been convinced that that was the case, even suggesting remedies and strategies to help. He knew that Paddy wanted to take him on a tour of Scout Tower but Mitch just kept putting it off and letting him down. It didn't sit well with him, but he just couldn't face it.

***

Paddy had continued to jabber away whilst he had been thinking thoughts of his lost love, but he started listening when he was dramatically shaken by the shoulders…

"We NEED YOU Mitch. Santa Paws, Shay, well he crash landed in the garden, and, well, we can sort out the Christmas deliveries tzu-wise. King Bailey is going to be Santa this year and some of us will help with the other roles, but no-one can fix the sleigh apart from YOU Mitch….NO ONE!"

"Calm down Paddy, am I really the only one that can help?"

He nodded, wide eyed and hopeful.

"Well, who's about, by the garden, in the Comforter Wing….is, erm, that Tzu Aroo singer there?"

Paddy shook his head sideways.

"Ok, give me a minute…"

Mitch grabbed a hammer, a screwdriver and a wrench, as well as a few nails, a pot of glue, a can of oil and some string.

"Quick, before Dada sees…"

The brothers jumped through their fairy door, landing with two burps, but Paddy's was bigger and louder.

"Oh Mitch, you didn't burp that bad after all!"

"Well, what do you know…it's a Christmas miracle!" he sniggered.

Chapter 12

Maisie strode in to the Party Room confidently, Stanley running behind her to keep up. There was a lot of chatter about the crash landing going on, but the band kept playing soft music in the background.

"Attention please," said Maisie, from the floor. She was so little that no-one could see or hear her. So, she jumped on the bar, "ATTENTION PLEASE," she shouted, but still no-one heard.

Stanley jumped on the bar himself, waved to Kemp, *Tzu Aroo* bass guitarist and pointed at Maisie. He nodded, turned to the band and they finished playing with Fergus the drummer adding a drum roll.

"Ladies and gentleman, I think a young lady would like to make an announcement...the floor is yours Maisie!" said Kemp.

Everyone looked at her and she giggled, but quickly regained her composure and stood tall on the bar, Stanley beside her.

"Following the crash tonight, we now have a Comforter Wing full of injured furs. They will be fine but they can't fly tonight and, well, the exciting news for us Tzus is that our very own King Bailey is going to be Santa Paws tonight!"

The crowd gasped and then cheered and applauded their King.

"But, we have something to fix, to set an example to the boys and girls of the world...you see, there are barely any toys for the homeless dogs who are in shelters and yet, back in our homes we have things that we could donate to help them...don't we?"

Tzus looked to each other and started to mumble in agreement.

"So my idea is that we all run home now through the fairy doors, grab a toy and pile everything up in the Welcome Room for Santa Bailey to deliver...are you in?"

"YES!" came the reply from the crowd!

A young tzu put her paw in the air and asked Maisie what sort of things they should bring.

"Any type of toy really my friend, remember this is for all sorts of dogs around the world so if it is too big or small or cumbersome for you, it will suit somefur".

Another tzu raised his paw and asked if it had to be their favourite toy.

"No, of course not, you keep your favourites, but maybe there is a toy that you just don't like the smell of but there is nothing wrong with it...well that's the sort of thing we need".

A tzu, one of a pair of twins, raised her paw and asked if it had to be your toy or whether it could be somefur else's toy.

Maisie gave her a stern look, "I think you know the answer to that don't you?" The querying tzu giggled and tickled her brother in the tummy.

An elder tzu raised his paw and asked if there was anything else that could be helpful, like a blanket or a pillow.

"Yes, remember there are elder tzus waiting for homes who would love something to cuddle up on or with".

The tzus applauded Maisie once again, impressed that one so little and young was also so clever.

"Well, then what are we waiting for?" she said. With that, tzus started to jump through the fairy doors, returning minutes later with teddy bears, tug toys, squeaky toys, blankets, soft pillows and tennis balls. They piled them up in the Welcome Room with excitement and pride, knowing that, this Christmas, they would have made a real difference to those less fortunate.

"Goodness, there's an awful lot of presents here!" said Maisie.

"There's been an awful lot of burps too!" Stanley sniggered, as the tzus returned through the fairy door wall.

Chapter 13

Paddy and Mitch had jumped back whilst Maisie was answering questions in the Party Room. They ran as fast as they could through the corridors to the Comforter Wing.

Paddy pushed the heavy wooden door open with a big smile on his face. He was so proud that he had finally got his big brother through to Tzu Kingdom after such a long absence. He knew Mitch was a regular here at one time but hadn't been around for a while.

"My big brother...Mitch," he announced.

"Mitch!" shouted Bailey, Coffee and Nancy as one, and rushed to say hello to their old friend.

"He didn't even get the big burps!" said Paddy, and everyone laughed. Except one glossy-furred tzu.

"Hey Mitchy," whispered Tuxie, sitting at the dressing table at the far side of the room, clearly upset.

"Oh, hi," said Mitch and turned to Paddy muttering under his breath, "you said she wasn't here..."

"Well she wasn't when I left..."

"Let's go get this sled thing fixed then," Mitch grumped as he went through to the patio, swinging his tool kit.

"What big burps?" said Tuxie to her friends, "he was never gassy around me..."

Paddy was confused; maybe the burps weren't the reason after all. Maybe, the reason he avoided Tzu Kingdom was Tuxie-related?

He went to follow Mitch but then noticed Tuxie sashaying after him and thought better of it.

Chapter 14

Stanley and Maisie returned to the Comforter Wing smiling and laughing, bursting to tell everyfur what had just happened.

They described the mounting pile of presents that were awaiting loading up on the Santa Paws' sleigh and how generous Tzu Kingdom had been.

"There's all sort of toys and lots of them are new," said Stanley.

"Plus blankets and pillows for older dogs to rest their old bones on," Maisie added.

Queen Coffee, King Bailey and Shay were so proud of everyfur and they hugged them all, whilst getting a huge tin of Christmas cookies from the kitchen for all to share.

"Well," said Shay, I think it is clear that you tzus understand the true meaning of Christmas. This is going to be the most wonderful year; I am just sad I won't be doing the delivering but I am happy to know that King B will be. Now, I think it's time to start assigning a few roles".

He sat up on the pile of beanbags and motioned to Binky, his assistant, to come and join him. Binky the Pekingese stood next to Shay, notebook and pencil in hand, and everyfur sat on beanbags to listen.

Shay explained what was needed – Santa Paws was in place but he had calculated that ten medium-sized tzus were needed in place of the six larger and stronger dogs that had pulled the sleigh for the real Santa Paws.

Stanley and Paddy put their paws up straight away and King Bailey nodded. They would be perfect.

"What about Kiki and Lola?" asked Queen Coffee to everyone's agreement.

"Them brothers would be good – Brickie, Hiro, Sammy and Percy – all fast and strong," suggested Paddy.

With two left to find, Stanley felt sad, "I wish Colin could do it," he sighed.

"Why can't he?" enquired Binky, looking confused.

"Colin has a disability, he walks with a limp and has a stick because of his wobbliness".

Shay's eyes lit up and he looked at his assistant and winked.

"That doesn't matter with Christmas magic Stanley – if he wants to be a sleigh dog than he can be – he will be able to fly just like the rest of you!" Binky enlightened him.

"Brilliant, this will make Colin's year! So we just need one more then..."

Bailey interrupted Binky the Elf Dog with some wise words, "I do think we need a tzu of experience to go with us..."

"Nancy can do it!" squealed Maisie and it made Nancy laugh.

"I am far too old for this sort of caper my sweet," she said, looking a little disappointed.

"If Colin can do it with a stick and his limp, then you can do it too".

"Nancy," Bailey interjected, "I was thinking we might stop for refreshments at Hotel Battenberg in Paris..."

Nancy jumped for joy – Paris held so many special memories for her and she had wanted to go to Hotel Battenberg again as a good friend of hers had moved there to be the Canine Concierge.

"OK!" Nancy exclaimed...let's do this!

***

"So," squeaked Binky, "we just need one more tzu to take my place. I have my lists, delivery information, route planner and all we need now is one small, organised tzu with leadership skills to complete my Christmas task".

Maisie smiled. "Perhaps that's a job for little me?" and twitched her nose in glee.

Chapter 15

Mitch was very grumpy indeed as he lined up his tools to fix the sleigh.

Tuxie, full of confidence earlier on stage, now hovered in the door feeling very small and unsure of herself. It had been ages since she had seen him and he didn't seem to want anything to do with her.

Brave as a lion, she spoke up.

"Mitchy, I've missed you".

"Oh, I didn't think you'd even notice".

"Well, of course I did...we had something special, you were always there helping me sound check and making sure everything was as it should be on stage and, well, then you just stopped and....well, I just thought you were busy with your new extended family and you'd be back once you settled them in and then Paddy starts coming through more and more and it just didn't make sense. And what's all this about your burping, it's no worse than any other tzu..."

Mitch stopped what he was doing and looked at the tzu of his dreams.

"But you took up with Kemp, he was always hanging about and I didn't think there was a place in the *Tzu Aroo* entourage for me any more".

"Is that what this is all about?" asked Tuxie. "Mitchy, Kemp is my new brother, same as Paddy is yours. Of course he was eager to help; he was a new addition to the band and to my family. Don't you know me better than that after all the years we have been together?"

Mitch felt terrible about thinking Tuxie would push him aside. Tuxie felt terrible that Mitch felt pushed out.

"Oh Tuxie, my beautiful songstress, please forgive me. There's been a terrible muddle and it's all my fault".

"No, it's my fault, I should have explained I..."

"Oh Tuxie, all this time, I really have missed you".

They hugged, then laughed and as Tuxie helped him fix the sleigh she asked him:

"Mitch, do you really have a gassy problem when you jump through?"

He burst out laughing. "No, I am the least burpy tzu I know and now I have to confess to Paddy!"

Chapter 16

Back in the Comforter Wing, Shay and Binky were briefing the Tzu Christmas team.

With no time to spare, Binky had been training Maisie in 'elfin duties' whilst Paddy and Stanley went to fetch Kiki, Lola, Brickie, Hiro, Sammy, Percy and Colin for sleigh-dog duty. They were all delighted to have been chosen for such an exciting task, especially Colin, who was bowled over by the thought of being able to fly like all the others, despite his disability. "I feel like a Paralympian," he exclaimed, tail wagging with enthusiasm.

Maisie had taken pages of notes in her little book and now, in her organised fashion, she was just repeating the instructions back to Binky, who was still a little dizzy from the crash and sipping apple juice from a beaker.

Having had a lot of experience of magic in her time in Tzu Kingdom, Maisie took it in her stride when Binky explained that the magic sprinkle dust was the key to the 'Team Christmas' success. He loaned her his satchel which sat neatly across her. Deftly, she dipped in to the bag and pulled out a pawful of rainbow coloured sprinkles. They looked just like the type you would put on a cake but they felt fizzy in her paw.

"That's the Christmas spell you can feel," said Binky.

As instructed, she sprinkled some on the Christmas list for the local area and it sparked and lit up. She turned around to the present sack that had been brought in for practice.

"Look inside," said Shay, smiling, having sprinkled a few of the strands in there himself.

She ran and poked her nose inside the sack. Inside some of the presents were glowing and, to her excitement and surprise, they twinkled and flew up in to her paws. She checked her list; the gift tags on the presents matched the dogs on the list. She checked it twice, just as Shay had told her.

"It's as simple as that," Binky said, "just as long as you keep your wits about you everything will be fine. Just don't eat the sprinkles or you will take flight yourself!"

Maisie smiled, she was going to ace this!

***

The sleigh-dog team were now back in the room and all had sat on beanbags two by two as there were larger dogs taking up six beanbags each recovering from the crash.

The two Santas, Shay and Bailey, took up position at the front of the assorted volunteers to brief them.

"Now then," said Shay, "the magic will take care of everything. It will steer you to the drop off points and Santa Bailey will deliver the gifts – it's your job to get him there safely and wait patiently whilst he does deliveries.

"The magic works by sprinkles, all you have to do is sprinkle some of the enchanted sugar strands over your heads and you will be able to fly and follow the Christmas route.

"But, please don't...Stanley, have you eaten some sprinkles there?"

"Erm, no," said Stanley, with rainbow sprinkles in his beard.

At this point, Kiki and Lola squealed and jumped up from their beanbag. They jumped again and grabbed Stanley's back paws – he was floating just above their heads!

"Oh my dog, oh my dog..." screamed Stanley as the girls pulled him back down to the ground.

Shay and Bailey stifled their giggles. Colin and Paddy put their heads in their paws and burst out laughing too!

"Don't panic Stanley," said Binky, "it'll wear off in a few minutes!"

He was embarrassed as the magic wore off and he came back down to earth. He was now floating just a few inches above the ground, thanks to the super fit Kiki and Lola, who had saved him from banging his head on the ceiling.

"Oh Stanley, you can't resist the sprinkles can you?" laughed Bailey.

Chapter 17

"It's ready furs...come see!" said Tuxie, turning tail and sauntering back out to the patio garden.

Everyone followed her to see a very proud Mitch standing by the repaired Christmas sleigh.

Shay sat down on the wall, overcome with emotion at the wonderful job that had seen his carriage returned to its usual glory.

"I promise I'll look after it," said Bailey, solemnly.

"Let's get this show on the road!" said Maisie, directing operations as she got every present and every tzu in place for the night's journey.

Everyone was ready and in their positions, but someone important didn't feel right. Bailey just didn't feel dressed for the occasion. He had decided to wear his favourite formal suit for the party tonight, but it just didn't look like he was Santa Paws in it.

The real Santa Paws was ahead of him.

"Just one final piece of magic to perform..." he said as he poured two enormous pawfuls of magic sprinkles over Bailey's head.

In front of their eyes, Bailey grew a little bit stouter, his beard grew a little thicker and his outfit turned into a big red coat with white trimmings, red trousers, sturdy black boots and a Santa hat. He looked like Bailey, but a Santa version.

Queen Coffee clapped her paws and sparkled with pride!

"Oh my lovely husband, look at you! You're King Bailey AND Santa Paws!"

Christmas wasn't cancelled after all.

Santa Bailey took his seat next to Maisie in the sleigh and, in front, ten tzus were ready to deliver the presents for all the dogs in the world through the Christmas Eve skies.

Chapter 18

As they ascended into the starry sky above the clouds, Tzu Kingdom got smaller and smaller. After a few minutes, Queen Coffee, Shay, Binky and the others were just dots and then they were out of view, as they soared higher and higher and faster and faster.

Within a few minutes, they had stopped off in Australia, New Zealand and Indonesia.

It wasn't long before they had their Canada stop and they all waved as they went over Coffee's house all covered in deep, deep snow.

Maisie had it completely under control and even the apartment blocks, like Phoebe's in New York, were no problem. She magic sprinkled the list; the presents sparkled and flew in to her paws. She passed them to Bailey who delivered them, magically, at the speed of light and then it was on to the next stop, Mexico, before heading to Europe.

In every country around the world, they stopped and left presents for the dogs who weren't as fortunate as them with the donations from Tzu Kingdom. Bailey was very proud as they made a difference to those who were waiting for homes in shelters and those who were lost and yet to be found.

The sleigh-dogs were amazing; smaller than the usual incumbents of the role but it didn't faze them. They kept on running through the sky, throwing magical, colourful sprinkles over each other so they could keep on flying.

They were about two thirds of the way through when King Bailey announced that it was time for a break and that he had a special stopover in mind before they started on the final leg of their journey.

"Tzus," he hollered to the flying furs in front of him, "see that sparkling building down there just on the River Seine, it has the biggest Christmas tree and a dog made out of fairy lights? That's Hôtel Battenberg so head for the roof and we will stop off and surprise our friend Louis, enjoy a banquet of amazing Christmas food and see how dogs should be treated!"

Chapter 19

Louis was enjoying a fine 'fête de Noël' at Hôtel Battenberg and he giggled at how very French he was these days. He loved his job here as '*Concierge Canine*' in what was one of the most dog-friendly hotels in the world. It had featured in 'WOOF!' magazine several times and played host to more and more celebrity dogs every week. His friend Colin had visited last summer with his famous dads and he had enjoyed dining with Colin in the hotel's doggy diner, 'Bark Bistro'.

Living in Paris was what his mummy had dreamed of all her life and, when the opportunity arose to manage a hotel there, they simply couldn't wait to pack up and go. He missed some of his old friends from Essex and he hadn't seen his old neighbour King Bailey for a long time. As a tzu, Louis could go to Tzu Kingdom through the fairy door behind the hotel's reception desk but, things had been so busy he hadn't had a moment to do so. He made a note in his head that he would pop through as soon as the Christmas rush was done with.

"Ahem..." came a bark from behind him. His ears pricked up – it sounded like Bailey but he dismissed that thought, putting it down to wishful thinking.

"Ahem, ahem, where's them 'saucisses' you promised me when I visited Mr Louis?"

He spun around and gasped. There, right in front of his eyes was Santa Paws. But he looked and sounded just like Bailey?

"It's me Louis – Bailey – I am Santa Paws this year, the real one had an accident in our garden and he's ok but, well, Coffee wouldn't let him or his team fly. I have a team of tzus and Nancy and Colin amongst them. I said we would stop here for refreshments!"

Well, not only could Louis not believe his eyes, now he couldn't believe his ears either. He scampered closer and peered into Santa Paws' eyes.

"Oh my dog, it's really you!"

Canine
Concierge
Hôtel Battenberg

Chapter 20

Catching up with each other, as old friends do, Louis and Bailey went up to the roof to lead the team down to 'Bark Bistro'.

"Look at that handsome tzu...would you look at that shiny coat!" said Kiki to Lola as Louis lifted little Maisie into the air and down from the sleigh seat.

It was true. Louis was glamorous, glossy-coated and athletic with a plume like a fountain of fur that brought him many an admirer. His smart, sophisticated uniform fitted him perfectly and gave him an air of authority and status. He was becoming quite the celebrity too as the hotel become renowned. He caught Kiki's eye and smiled as he sashayed past them to the hotel's roof entrance.

"Ok, follow me," he said, "the party has finished and most dogs have gone to their suites to wait for Santa Paws – not knowing that he is here himself - but there's plenty of gourmet snacks for you still in 'Bark Bistro'".

"There's vol-au-vents filled with every flavour you could dream of, there's saucisses, of course, there's frogs legs, fromage and, oh, who wants to try 'escargot'?"

"What's that?" asked Paddy.

"It's a French delicacy, I think you will like it..." said Louis, passing a plate to the boys to try.

Paddy took a pawful and shoved them in his mouth and almost immediately spat them out!

"Bleurghhhhhh," he said, "disgusting!"

But Stanley persevered, ‘no worse than some of Mama’s cooking,’ he thought to himself.

"What are they made of Louis?” he asked politely.

"Snails…” said Louis, nonchalantly, "maybe try some of the salmon bites,” he suggested, "they are good for giving you a shiny coat”.

Lola and Kiki ran over, if they were going to get a coat like Louis they were in! Stanley and Paddy followed, feeling a little queasy about the snails.

Chapter 21

King Bailey had always felt fatherly towards Maisie from the first night he met her and, whilst the others were eating and chatting he took a quiet little Maisie by the paw to show her something special. She loved the stories of Tzu Royalty but he knew she was mesmerised by his story and, especially, his romance with and wedding to Queen Coffee. Paris was quite special to them and he wanted to share it with his elf, to thank her for all her hard work in organising the present deliveries.

They sneaked outside to the front of the hotel and stood in the light that shone from the enormous fairy-lights-dog as a dusting of snow fell around them.

"Look," he said, "over there, see that building well, that is the Eiffel Tower where Coffee and I married. There were troubled times in Tzu Kingdom and we eloped, Coffee and I, so we could return and rule paw-in-paw. Louis performed the ceremony and we had just three guests. We all came over here afterwards for a celebration dinner – that's why Nancy wanted to return and has flown with us tonight. She'll be asleep all Christmas Day I would imagine!"

"Do you see the bright and colourful lights up and down the River Seine and on the boats? Beautiful aren't they...I just thought you would like to see before we finished our amazing Christmas adventure".

Maisie was quite overcome with the emotion of it all and her eyes were wide with wonderment.

Suddenly, she flung her paws around Bailey's neck and hugged him tight.

"Merry Christmas King Santa Bailey...we all love you so much".

***

They returned to find the tzus ready to depart. They thanked Louis for his hospitality and the sleigh-dogs raced each other up the stairs, the four brothers first, followed by Kiki and Lola with Stanley, Maisie and Paddy behind them.

Bailey, Louis, Nancy and Colin walked slowly behind them. The older tzus still had a little Christmas Magic in their fur, but were a little slower and looking forward to being covered in magic sprinkles to complete their journey.

"Promise not to leave it too long before we see you in Tzu Kingdom Louis. In fact, why don't you come through for our New Year's Day Breakfast in the café? It would be a delight to see you, it's not a morning where you see any humans too early!" said Bailey.

"Looking forward to it already," said Louis, warmly shaking Bailey's paw.

Santa Bailey climbed back in to the sleigh seat, everyone threw magic sprinkles over each other and they climbed into the night sky once again, until Louis and Hôtel Battenberg were hidden behind the snow filled clouds.

Chapter 22

They touched down in Tzu Kingdom just as night was turning into morning. Queen Coffee was waiting at the patio doors with the slightly dazed Team Christmas, who were all a little better and ready to go home.

"I still don't think Shay is up to flying Bailey," said Coffee, concern etched on her face.

"No, no need. I've already thought this through…" said Bailey, winking at his lovely wife.

Shay, Binky, Custard, Marmalade, Teddy, Blondie, Marley and Clapton took up their positions as the tzu team disembarked so the real team could get ready for their short flight home.

The real Santa Paws paused as he climbed aboard. "Thank you my friends, thank you. This has been an amazing Christmas and you've all been so kind and as brave as lions. Be good, maybe I will see you another year.

"Come on team, it's home time – back to Santa Paws Land!"

The tzus all waved until they disappeared behind the stars and Coffee looked at her tired but excited friends. It was time for them to all jump through the fairy doors, but she thought a little more partying wouldn't hurt!

"One more quick dance in the Party Room with Tuxie and Tzu Aroo, then straight home for every one of you.

"How will Bailey get home Coffee?" asked a concerned Lola.

"He's going to guide the sleigh home and drop them all in their own world and then he will…"

"...come back through the fairy doors with a little timey-wimey magic?" finished King Bailey, now stood next to Coffee, dressed in his suit, as dapper as he had been at the start of the party.

"After all these dog years, this place still amazes me!" laughed Nancy.

Stanley's eyes lit up, a thought occurring to him.

"So if the Christmas magic is done, does that mean we can eat the rest of the sprinkles?"

***

They all returned to the Party Room to finish the evening with a song and a dance. Mitch helped Tuxie up on to the stage as Paddy looked on, wondering what the story was between his brother and the stunning singer.

"Well furs," said Tuxie, "this is gonna be the last one from me for a while. Don't forget we start auditions for new band members on New Year's Day so make sure you practise over Christmas week!"

"I have one little song to sing to you to celebrate this very special Tzu Christmas...hit it boys!"

1...2...3 said Fergus and hit the drums and Tuxie started to sing...

"Santa Bailey, stick a squeaky under the tree

For me...

Been an awful good Tzu

Santa Bailey, hurry with my chew toy tonight"

Tzu
Aroo

Chapter 23

Back home in Belfast on Christmas Day, Mitch and Paddy were lying on the floor after eating a plate each of turkey, sausages and bacon.

"I couldn't eat another thing this afternoon!" Paddy said.

It had been a great day and everyone had enjoyed each other's company and loved their presents. Santa Paws had left some lovely toys for them and they were happy to know that Santa Bailey had done such a great job after stepping in at the last minute.

"Listen to this amazing news," said the youngest human brother, quoting from his news feed.

"Astonishing scenes all over the world as piles of toys were left at every dog shelter along with blankets, tennis balls and pillows with a little label that said 'Love from Santa Paws'".

The older human brother read the story over his shoulder.

"That's fantastic," he said and then, thoughtfully, "maybe we should sort out some of our old stuff tomorrow and give it to charity?"

They nodded in agreement.

"We did that! I am proud of you little brother, I really am," said Mitch.

Paddy smiled a really happy smile and dreamt of all the adventures yet to come in Tzu Kingdom.

Tzu Kingdom

Santa Paws' Invitation

From the desk of Santa Paws
The Palace of Santa Paws
Santa Paws Land

3rd February 2017

King Bailey of Tzus
Tzu Kingdom
Via the Fairy Doors

My dear friend Bailey

Thank you for saving Christmas for all the dogs of the world!

Woofs can never even begin to express the extent of my gratitude for what you did this past Christmas by standing in for me after the crash landing in Tzu Kingdom.

I am pleased to say that we are now all fully recovered, but only thanks to the love and care we received in your world.

You and your team delivered every dog his or her gift exactly as planned, plus the additional gifts for the shelter dogs around the world.

I continue to be enormously impressed and humbled at the work Queen Coffee and your good self do in using your Kingdom for good and your tireless work in rescuing tzus-less-fortunate. You are an example to all of us dogs.

Dear King, I would like to invite the youngsters who formed the 2016 #TeamChristmas to visit my Palace and explore Santa Paws Land as my honoured guests at the beginning of December this year, just as things start to get very busy and, of course, when the baking starts in earnest!

So, I will ask Elf-Dog Binky and my Palace Manager Embry to organise a date with dear Queen Coffee and I look forward to welcoming Stanley, Paddy, Kiki, Lola, Sammy, Percy, Brickie, Hiro and, of course, your little elf Maisie to my world.

Please advise them to wrap up warm as I have a special treat in store at the end of the tour...

With a paw full of love to Coffee and you dear friend,

Shay

Chapter 1

Maisie shih tzu was so excited as she waited for the others in the Welcome Room. She had been sitting with Lennon for ages chatting away, telling him all about the night she was King 'Santa' Bailey's elf-dog when Shay, the Soft Coated Wheaten Terrier and the real Santa Paws, had crash landed in the gardens at Tzu Kingdom and King Bailey took his place with his own team delivering the presents to all the dogs in the world.

He knew the entire story, he had been there on the night, but Lennon was a kind old soul and he wasn't going to burst her bubble.

Four little burps from the fairy door wall made them look up. Sammy and Percy had jumped through their door just as Brickie and Hiro had jumped through theirs. Excitedly, they ran to Maisie and Lennon.

"Oh my dog, it's finally here!" Sammy exclaimed, jumping up and down and taking his brothers' paws making them skip around in a circle. Maisie giggled as she watched them.

"We're here too!" squealed Lola and Kiki as they ran to join the fun.

As instructed by Queen Coffee, they had all dressed up warm and wore snow boots, long coats, scarves, mittens and hats.

"What's occurring?" said a gruff voice from behind them. Paddy had jumped down from Scout Tower, where he had just been to check on things before he left for the day. He took his Chief Scout role very seriously and had earned the respect of everyone, including the King and Queen of Tzus.

Maisie giggled. "What are you wearing under your hat?" she queried.

"Ear muffs," he replied, wearing a sensible face. "I get problems with me ears so Mam said I mustn't get a chill on them or they'll hurt. Mam knows these things so I'm not taking any chances, I had to have them de clogged at the V.E.T. last year and I don't fancy a day trip there for me Christmas present, thank you very much!"

She considered this response and thought that was very prudent indeed. Chief Scout Paddy was far from a fool and listening to his mam was, she mused, an excellent idea.

"Are we all here?" Brickie enquired, eager to start the walk down the special corridor that led to Santa Paws Land. King Bailey would be here any minute to bark-code it open for them and they would be met by Binky, Santa Paws' Elf whom they had met before, and Embry, the golden fur who managed Santa's Palace and estate.

"Just one tzu missing," Hiro laughed.

"STAN!" they all shouted.

Chapter 2

King Bailey and Queen Coffee could be heard walking down the corridor, chatting and laughing, ready to send the group on their way.

"What do we do now? We can't go without Stan!" asked Percy, nervously.

"Has anyone got a café grab bag of doughnuts?" Maisie asked.

Of course, they all did. Bags of doughnuts and sandwiches for the journey down the corridor were held in every set of paws. Maisie however, had been busy chatting to Lennon and forgotten to get one.

"Paddy, can I borrow one please?"

Slightly, grudgingly, Paddy pawed over a doughnut to his friend. A jam-filled one, covered in sugar.

Maisie barked at the fairy door wall, opening Stanley's door and waved the doughnut in front of it, wafting the smell towards his house.

"Thanks Paddy, here's your doughnut back".

He ate it, thinking it might not fit back in the grab bag now it had been exposed to daylight.

They waited, worrying as they heard the royal pawsteps getting closer and anxious that they might miss their time slot, or have to go without Stanley.

"BURP!"

"Morning all," laughed Stanley, hurriedly putting on his woolly tartan hat and mittens. "Busy time of year for Mama and me! We worked all day and then a friend of ours has come to stay to enjoy the Edinburgh Christmas fun so I have been supervising and, well, it was just a late night I suppose. Not late, am I?"

They all shook their heads, stifling their giggles.

"I'm just glad you are here my hero!" Maisie planted a kiss in his beard, and he blushed.

The group was complete, it was time to go to visit Santa Paws.

Chapter 3

"Morning, my young furs!" Queen Coffee sung, looking on proudly at the warmly dressed shih tzus. "This is going to be a very exciting day for you. It's going to be tremendous fun I know, but make sure you stick together in your pairs and Stanley, Paddy and Maisie as a trio please".

King Bailey stepped forward. "Now, I know I don't really have to say this but, it's best to be clear. You are all going to Santa Paws Palace as representatives of Tzu Kingdom and, well, Coffee and I are more than happy to let you represent us all and the high reputation of this world. I hope...no... I am **sure** none of you will let us down and that every tzu will be on their very best behaviour".

"Now, Paddy you are the most senior tzu in the group today so please look after them".

"Not a problem KB. Consider it done," he nodded, respectfully to the King as he continued his briefing.

"OK, so I am going to bark the corridor open now. Embry and Binky will be there waiting. It's quite a walk so pace yourselves; you don't want to be worn out before you get there.."

"Oh, I have packed some gifts to take through, if you could pass them to Embry and say hello, she really is a dear friend of mine," Coffee interrupted, passing boxes to the girls to take.

"Thank you darling, it's important to say thank you to your hosts. Well, I must ask you to cover your ears please, this is a secret bark code. I see you've already covered your ears Paddy, what lovely muffs, very sensible".

Paddy grinned, King Bailey recognised style when he saw it.

They lined up, with their paws over their long ears, as the king barked and the door swung open, magically.

"Have a lovely time!" Coffee, Bailey and Lennon wished them as they jumped through and entered a long tunnel with no end to be seen.

Chapter 4

The tunnel got colder as they walked along, holding paws with their partner but they were toasty warm, so it didn't matter.

At first, the tunnel was made of red brick with a raised flooring of wooden boards but then they turned a corner and it became lighter, brighter and the smells of sausages and doughnuts from Tzu Kingdom gave way to smells of Christmas dinner, cinnamon and gingerbread.

The bricks were white now and the floor too, with snow. Flakes of ice danced around in front of their faces as they walked along and the nearer they got, the denser the snow became.

They heard music, Christmas songs, familiar from their own family Christmases.

"Oh, I love this one!" Stanley shouted, as he started to sing one of his favourite songs that he would sing with Mama in the kitchen as they had their work breaks.

"I know it too!" Paddy piped up. "Let's sing it!"

"Me too! But I will just listen to you boys, I want to look out for Binky".

And so this is Christmas
Fur weak and fur strong
Fur rich and the poor Tzus
The world is so wrong
And so happy Christmas
Fur black and fur white
Fur brindle, red & gold ones
Let's pitch in and fight

A very Merry Christmas
And a happy new year
Let's hope fur a Paw Stomp

With the ones we hold dear

Maisie enjoyed the singing, reflecting on how very 'Tzu Kingdom' those words were and that, maybe, it was being played for their arrival.

Then they turned a corner and, without doubt, they had arrived at Santa Paws Palace.

It was enormous, towering above them, the walls covered in twinkling lights, with hundreds of little star shaped windows, leading to clusters of turrets and with a large bow wrapped around its circumference.

Although it was set within deep snow with snowflakes all around, it didn't feel cold at all.

A big set of old wooden doors opened slowly, at the end of a covered walkway to the palace and there, with her paws outstretched, stood a tall, sophisticated, curly furred caramel poodle with a tiny Pekingese right beside her.

"Maisie!" screeched Elf-Dog Binky and ran forward for a hug.

"Binky, oh I have so been looking forward to seeing you again! Well, we all have! Haven't we?"

Everyone gathered around each other, hugging and laughing whilst they chatted about the success of Christmas 2016. It had been quite a triumph, arising from that terrible moment when it seemed like no dogs would get their presents.

As they walked in, they told Binky that King Bailey of Tzus was well but looking forward to putting his paws up with Queen Coffee this Christmas and waving at Santa Paws as he went over Tzu Kingdom. Binky promised that, if they were ahead of schedule, they would stop in for a quick visit at the Tzu Kingdom party, parking properly this time!

He introduced them to Embry, she was from Ontario in Canada, not far from where Coffee lived.

"Do you know our Queen Coffee?" Lola quizzed.

"Well, we have bumped in to each other on occasion, mainly at market on the weekends when we help with chores. We wink and natter, if only our humans knew what we did!"

She smiled kindly; Lola wasn't surprised they were friends.

"We have gifts for you, Coffee sent them, with the compliments of Tzu Kingdom," said Kiki, holding out her box as Maisie and Lola did the same.

Embry gasped as she opened each box in turn. In the first box were doughnuts that the Tzu Queen had baked, glistering with gold sprinkles, in the second some scented room candles and in the final box some vintage marrowbone sauce, brewed by King Bailey himself.

"Thank you dear tzus, Santa Paws will love these gifts. Something nice to eat, something to help us relax and something to give extra flavour to the Christmas table for Team Christmas when our mission is done! And all home-made! What a delight!"

Maisie made a little note in her book of what Embry had said so she could report back.

"Well, I think it's time to start the tour so let's get inside and get things going. Quick like snow bunnies!"

The youngsters all looked at each other, happy that they were going on this wonderful adventure.

Other Dog Worlds
Bark Code Access
Only

Chapter 5

The tzus arrived in the Entrance Hall of the palace to be greeted by a table full of juice, warm vanilla milk, Stollen and gingerbread cookies.

Around them was a small team of small dogs – bichons, chihuahuas, lhasa aphsos, border terriers, westies, and pugs as well as mix-breed dogs in their elf uniforms. They bustled around the room, shaking paws as they met their guests and handing out drinks and plates. They were so pleased to meet the Christmas 2016 team, they had heard a lot about them and they were interested to know what role each had fulfilled on the previous year's delivery flight.

However, Brickie was perplexed.

"How comes they are all different breeds, shapes and sizes?"

"Well, perhaps I can explain?" said a squeaky voice from a tiny Chinese Crested with big eyes. "Zoey...pleased to meet you"..

They all gathered around her; they were desperate to know.

***

Team Christmas is an international, cross-breed organisation consisting of all sorts of dogs with different skills and abilities, pulled from dog worlds and kingdoms across the world. It's one of the oldest dog institutions and it has existed for thousands of dog years.

So, the team will always hail all sorts of dogs, working to the best of their ability. As you saw last year, SP's Sleigh Dogs included dogs like Teddy and Blondie the labradoodles and you have seen that elfs tend to be smaller breeds helping to get Santa Paws ready for the big day and others working on toys, clothes, tech, treats, beds, baskets, experiences...pretty much anything a pooch could dream of!

If you look out for him, you will see that your friend Gizmo Goggins the Tzu is working in the gingerbread bakery, following his stint as manager of Tzu Bakery. He applied last year and we are delighted to have him join the team this year! Dogs tend to be part of the team for a few years at a time and have heaps of fun, but it is exhausting!

Team Christmas, in the main, changes almost every year so if any of you ever want to do your bit for Christmas, well you just need to approach your King or Queen and they will speak to us here.

Soft Coated Wheaten Terrier Shay, the current holder of the office of Santa Paws, he's the latest in a long line of incumbents to take the oath and lead us so we can make Christmas special for all the dogs of the world for a term of up to ten years. This is Shay's eighth Christmas as Santa Paws and, even now, he's looking around for a potential successor and he or she will take over soon, allowing Shay to enjoy a relaxing retirement of many years. This is only Embry's third year as Palace Manager, so she will, in the next couple of years, settle in a new Santa Paws before taking some time herself.

We all have our own homes and our own worlds to enjoy of course, but being part of Team Christmas well, it's something special.

The tzus looked at each other, thinking about what they had been told and wondering if they would ever be part of #TeamChristmas.

"OK!" Binky hollered, "who's for a trip to the factory floor?"

Chapter 6

It was vast!

The factory took up the whole of the East Wing and was spread over five floors.

On the ground floor, traditional toys were made and piles of stuffies, balls, kongs and squeakies were being produced and placed in to large carts for quality control inspections.

On the first floor was Technical. Expert dogs were working with detailed blue prints to make FitBarks, illuminated collars and electric cars.

The second floor was filled with beds, baskets and beyond. Carpenters were fitting together large pieces of wood to make sturdy beds; soft beds were being sewn together and blankets were being knitted at an impressive rate.

Outfitting and apparel was burgeoning on the third storey! The modern dog cared about their appearance and they were elbow to elbow, stitching, sewing, knitting and altering their orders, laughing as they went and hanging the finished clothing on rails.

On the top floor was the kitchen and there were biscuits with cheese, gravy bones, carob bars and gingerbreads being baked and loaded carefully in to Tupperware and put in to a cold room for storage.

"I could never work so close to the kitchen Paddy," Stanley confessed, "it's bad enough when you get a waft from the café in Scout Tower when you open the hatch!"

"You're not wrong there Stan!" he replied, wondering if he could politely polish off a doughnut soon, the smell was making him peckish.

"I could just lose myself in those beds and have a lovely snooze," Hiro sighed, thinking it had been a long day already with so much to take in.

"Look at all the dresses!" Maisie gasped, gabbing Lola and Kiki's paws.

"I love those ties," Kiki exclaimed, "maybe we can get them for our boyfriends for Christmas? Louis would look divine in the striped one, maybe stars for Stanley Maisie and, Lola, the checks for Mac!"

"Sammy, Brickie, we could play football here all day," Percy yelled, knowing what he would put on his Christmas list and thinking back to the many happy hours the four of them had spent playing football with Maisie when they had first been rescued and were all living happily together for some months in the Comforter Wing.

"OK. There is some free time at the end of the day when we split you in to teams for a special something, so you can come back here and visit any floor you wish. But now, let's move on to 'Quality and Despatch'. West Wing," Binky shouted, indicating for the team to follow him through the central atrium.

As they walked they could hear a rolling sound, like a train and they looked down and, through a glass floor they could see the gifts they had seen made were now in the carts being wheeled along by big strong breeds.

Chapter 7

As they strolled in to 'Quality and Despatch' they were met by a wonky-toothed cross terrier called Pixie. She was ever so dainty, and the tooth gave her a distinct and unique look that made her super confident.

"Don't be fooled by her size team...Pixie runs a very tight ship here!" Binky advised, cheekily.

She smiled at him and winked.

"May I ask you all to sign in for elf and safety reasons please?" she said, firmly and efficiently, pointing at a visitor book.

Once they had all signed the book, they followed her.

"ATTENTION!" she blasted across the floor and whistled through her wonky tooth, in the unlikely event that they hadn't heard her shout.

'Despatch' was made up of mainly large dogs lifting, sorting and packing gifts into boxes however, when Pixie yelled, they all stood to attention and the place fell quiet so all that could be heard was the hum of the conveyor belt. You could have heard a cookie drop.

"Oh, she's good," said Kiki, in admiration.

"Team," Pixie began, "these are our VIF guests today and I would like you to make them welcome and show them around our operation here. For those who don't know, this was #TeamChristmas2016, they took over when Santa Paws had his little mishap in Tzu Kingdom".

The furs gasped and broke into a spontaneous round of applause and cheers, resulting in some considerable blushing amongst the visitors.

A smart young morkie ran forward from a door on their left, with a whistle hung around his neck and a bouncy ball in his paws.

"Me is Beckham, Quality Controller, pleased to meet you...follow me...me have to test all the balls!"

They ran after him, over to a small netted court area. Beckham threw them a ball each.

"It's great fun this job but it takes a fit dog that's for sure! Every ball has to be bounced ten times and then given a paw stamp and loaded in to a box to be taken over to Despatch".

"We are looking for a good bounce each time from the first to the tenth".

They all tried it out and loved bouncing the balls. They sampled three each, found two rejects amongst them and placed them in to the recycling box.

They laughed as Brickie and Maisie did a few trick shots, remembering the fun they had in the Comforter Wing.

Pixie arrived at the gate.

"Come on, time to go to Despatch".

Chapter 8

Maisie squeezed Stanley's paw as they walked in. She loved organising things and that's what made her such an excellent Elf-Dog to Santa Bailey last year.

She had reorganised Tzu Gallery and was now Curator and she was halfway through her refurbishment of Tzu Library. To be met by labelled shelves in labelled aisles full of labelled gifts was a dream come true.

Organisation wasn't Stanley's thing and you could tell by the state of his locker in Tzu Kingdom's Scout Tower but, all that mattered to him was that his stuff was in there somewhere if he rummaged for it and that inside the door was a picture of him with Mama, Dad and Granny, another of him with Paddy in their uniforms from when he qualified as a Scout and a heart-shaped one of Maisie wearing her favourite pink and white party dress, her fur tied in sparkly fur clips.

"Hi Team Tzu!" enthused a large black German Shorthair Pointer with a big smile as he threw his paws around them in turn, "I'm Finn, Senior Packer”.

He was very bouncy, and they all laughed, his enthusiasm was infectious, and it couldn't fail to bring a smile to your face.

"Finn, how do you keep control of every fur and all the parcels?" asked a wide-eyed Maisie.

"Well, this whole operation depends on our team getting all the parcels in the right place for the Elf-Dogs to deliver with Santa Paws. It is down to precision timing so every dog in here makes a commitment to work hard in the run up to

Christmas and there's no time for slackness as we just can't be late!"

"There's a lot of collies here," said Lola, thoughtfully, to Finn.

"Indeed. They are excellent at putting all the gifts on the right shelf, they literally herd them to their correct position".

"How does the magic occur?" Paddy questioned, fascinated by what was going on before his very eyes.

"I can't give any secrets away, but there's a dormant spell put on every gift. It activates once sprinkled with Christmas magic and, after he's checked it twice, it will marry up with the spell on Santa Paws' list as the magic sprinkles are sprinkled on that too. Finn Dog can say no more!" he laughed.

Before there were any more questions, Pixie and Binky reappeared.

"OK, time to go off to the offices tzus..."

"Oh no..." came the response, with some very disappointed faces.

"...where Embry is waiting for you...as is Santa Paws".

Chapter 9

Binky walked them back through the atrium and turned right to the East Wing, where Embry was waiting to show them around.

"Thank you sweet Binky, what an excellent job you are doing. Would you mind just popping through to the West Wing and checking on lunch?"

"Not at all Em," he said, skipping off to supervise lunch, thinking he might need to do a little quality control.

"Are you all enjoying yourselves?" Embry asked.

They all nodded, still tremendously excited about their visit, although they were a little tired and hungry now.

"Well, this is the office suite so please take a gingerbread and a warm vanilla milk to keep you going until lunch".

They didn't need telling twice and helped themselves to refreshments, returning swiftly to hear what Embry had to say.

"May I introduce you all to Jock please. He's a Scottie and he is Office Supervisor here, reporting directly to me".

Jock wheeled himself forward, with a clipboard and pencil on his lap that he picked up in his front paws once he had parked his wheels.

"Which one of you is Paddy Boo?"

Paddy blushed as everyone looked at him and he slowly put his paw in the air.

"Oh Paddy, Chief Scout, it's an honour to meet you! You will find a lot of synergy in what we do here with your work in Scout Tower".

Paddy felt embarrassed at being picked out in the line-up, but also very proud. But he decided the limelight should be shared.

"Well, that's great Jock thanks and, erm, this is Stanley and he's my deputy".

That was better, the two of them, together, Stanley having been pushed to the left side of his best friend, just like they always stood, in alphabetical order.

They grinned, not sure what they should do now.

"Well, let's show you how things work in here," Jock continued.

He showed them how, over three floors, the Elf-Dogs processed every 'Dear Santa Paws' letter that arrived, keeping records of every single known dog in the world as well as rescue centres, foster homes and shelters.

"...and which one of you is Maisie?" Jock enquired.

"I am! I am!" declared Maisie, showing none of Paddy's bashfulness.

"Well, Maisie, it is thanks to your example last year that we now have a separate section that deals with all the donations that more fortunate dogs, from all worlds and kingdoms give us, so we can share them amongst those dogs who are, shall we say, less fortunate. Santa Paws Shay will be able to leave gifts at all the shelters and foster homes over the world".

Maisie smiled, broadly, as she got a round of applause from the rest of her friends. Stanley beamed with pride at his girlfriend's acclaim. She deserved it. It had been completely her idea.

Something had occurred to Kiki and she raised her paw.

"Jock, I just wondered where dogs get sorted in to 'naughty or nice'?"

"Well Kiki, that's done by Santa Paws himself on the advice of the most senior elf dogs but, do you want to see where we deal with the naughty list?"

They did. They were eager to know what a naughty dog looked like, what you had to do to be naughty enough to get on the list and wondered what they got for Christmas. Maybe a bag of mouldy sprouts, a lump of coal or a stinky sock.

"Follow me to the department responsible," Jock smirked, taking off his chair brake, turning around and riding past all the desks piled high with letters and with elf-dogs working diligently, yet politely looking up to say hello. He wheeled on and on and on to the very back of the room, zig-zagging through sections until he arrived at a small table and chair pushed up against a brick wall in a corner, with no staff, lamp or Christmas decoration in sight. He spun around and pulled his brakes on next to the desk that bore nothing but a sign with its name.

"There. The naughty dog department". He pointed at the sad looking sign.

"But there's nothing here?" Stanley stated, making an obvious point.

"There's good reason for that," said a voice from behind them, Embry had followed them down, "there are no naughty dogs, just bad owners".

She smiled. "Come on team, thank you Jock. But I think it is time to see Santa Paws and learn about the big surprise he has in store for you all”.

Chapter 10

The team followed Embry up the stairs. As they arrived on the top floor, Binky jumped out of the lift.

"BOO!"

They jumped and giggled at him. He was a funny little fellow.

"Now," Embry began, "Santa is very busy at the moment and he has arranged a very special surprise for you and he's going to show you something quite amazing. I know you have lots of questions, but he has only an hour to spend with you all, so let's all make the best of the time. In just three weeks, Santa Paws will take to the skies and deliver presents to every known dog in the world, so we mustn't eat in to his schedule".

"After he has told you about the surprise we will go down to the lounge for lunch and...well...I won't say any more for fear of spoiling it...but if you do have questions, I will answer whatever I can over lunch and, if you do want to visit some of the departments for a more in-depth look, just let me know".

Paddy spoke on behalf of the team. "Thank you Embry, we understand".

She turned to a beautiful multi-coloured glass door with bells and lights that led to the official office of Santa Paws and tapped.

"Come on in '2016 #TeamChristmas'!" boomed a voice from the other side of the door.

Binky and Embry pushed open the doors and there, sat at his desk in a red and white cardigan, peering over his spectacles and wearing an enormous welcoming smile, he was.

Santa Paws himself.

Chapter 11

Every one of Santa Paws' guests were woofless. His office was warm, welcoming and full of twinkling lights.

Behind him was a line of Christmas trees, packed with baubles, candy canes and topped with stars.

On each wall was a clock counting down to Christmas Eve, currently on 20 days and a few hours.

Something caught Maisie's eye and she ran to the wall, grabbing Stanley's paw on the way to show him. "Look!"

There, in chronological order, were tiny pawtraits of every Santa Paws that had ever been and it went back hundreds and hundreds of years. They worked back from Seamus.

2010 – present SEAMUS Soft Coated Wheaten Terrier

2002 – 2009 MEGHAN King Charles Spaniel

1997 – 2001 RUFUS Old English Sheepdog

1990 – 1996 COCO Miniature Schnauzer

1981 – 1989 CORNELIUS Pug

1971 – 1980 TARA Lhasa Apso

"Look Stan, Tara was a Lhasa – that's almost like being Tzu! Maybe one day, you or I could be Santa Paws?"

"Oh wow, imagine, I mean just imagine," he replied, bowled over by the beautiful palace he stood in and wondering what it would be like.

"I wouldn't want to be Santa Paws though Stanley if it meant we were apart. I would only want to do it together or not at all".

They squeezed paws and smiled.

"Paw-in-Paw like Coffee and Bailey," Stanley responded.

"Ahem," coughed Paddy, "are you two being soppy and romantic?"

He raised his eyebrows and laughed. "Come on, Santa is taking us to a special secret room!"

"Follow Santa Paws," said Embry ushering them down a corridor that led from his office, following the others, "quick like snow bunnies!"

They all giggled, that was like one of Queen Coffee's phrases, but with snow. It must be a Canadian thing.

"Where are we going Paddy?" Maisie asked.

"The Magic Room," came the answer.

Chapter 12

The guests arrived at the entrance to a room, accompanied by Santa Paws, Binky and Embry. In front of them was a sealed door, with no handle, bolt or lock.

They looked all around but couldn't see any way of getting in. The whole wall was sealed in glitter and it sparkled so bright you could only look at it for a few seconds before you had to close your eyes or look away.

"Ready?" Santa said, "time for a triple-lock-unlock".

Embry and Binky walked to the door and together they placed their front left paws on the door in the shape of a triangle. It glowed bright and a door slowly opened to reveal a room full of glass boxes containing sprinkles. The room was warm, and the walls glowed.

"This is where we cultivate the magic, all year, and we release it on Christmas Eve, when it's ready to activate. There's enough to deliver all the gifts to the dogs of the world and a little extra, just in case," Santa Paws explained.

"But," he said, "we always do a couple of test flights around this time of year, just to make sure everything is working OK. It won't go all around the world but there's enough for a few short flights. Now, how would you like to accompany Binky and me on the practice runs?"

They could not believe their ears! They jumped up and down with excitement as if they were puppies. Last year they had been sleigh-dogs but now, they were going to get a fun ride!

Santa Paws loved to see their excitement. He explained that two of the Sleigh Dogs would pull them along as there were no presents to carry and they could all choose a location to visit. They would go in pairs, and Paddy, Maisie and Stanley in a trio.

Embry explained that lunch would be ready now, so the first pair would head off with Santa and Binky, whilst she led the others to the lounge for lunch. They would return and swap.

Percy and Sammy were the first to fly and had chosen to go to the island of Tenerife in Spain. Kiki and Lola would be next, and they would pay a visit to The Maldives to see a little sunshine. Brickie and Hiro just wanted to go to the Scottish Highlands, a place they had been on holiday in the summer with their family and somewhere they wouldn't mind moving their family to.

Paddy, Stanley and Maisie weren't fussed, they just wanted to ride in the sky, so they said they would just follow their noses when it was their turn.

They waved Percy and Sammy take off and disappear high in to the sky and skipped behind Embry down to lunch.

This was one of the most exciting days ever.

***

The lunch table was exquisite and a lot like a Tzu Kingdom party. There were sausages, a selection of cheese and lots of muffins but the centrepiece was a two-metre-tall Gingerbread House, decorated with icing, jellies and sprinkles. Over the top was an enchanted snow cloud that constantly dusted the house with icing sugar.

"How does this work?" they all asked, looking all over to see if there was a switch, lever or strings.

Stanley was a little reluctant to eat the sprinkles as last year he had munched away on a couple only to find himself take off, magically, powered by their enchantment, and rescued by the girls. He was still embarrassed about it.

"They're not enchanted sprinkles, don't worry young Stan," Embry had assured him, stroking his furrowed brow.

But they said they would save it until they had all been on their sleigh-ride. With that, Percy and Sammy returned. Outside the arched door Santa Paws and Binky waved. Embry hurried Kiki and Lola off for their excursion, knowing that Santa would soon need to get back to work and there was no time to spare.

Once again, the sleigh took off with a whoosh and disappeared in to the sky, leaving Sammy and Percy to tell their friends what they had seen and how they had done a loop-the-loop over France and waved to their friend Louis Battenberg at his hotel on the River Seine.

They shared out some sausages, pleased to see that Santa Paws Land also had a gravy fountain in which to dip and then a gust of wind, a flurry of snow and the girls had returned. They disembarked, giggling with Binky and making him blush as they shook the sand out of their fur.

It was Brickie and Hiro's turn. They ran to the door, high-pawing Kiki and Lola on the way and once more, whoosh, off towards the Highlands of Scotland.

"It won't be long until it's our turn," Maisie smiled at Stanley and Paddy, "make sure you have your mittens on, coats done up and hats pulled down so they don't fly off! Paddy, your ear muffs need to be on straight, we don't want you getting sore ears," and she straightened them up herself, just to be sure.

In the distance they could see them returning from their short flight.

"Time to go!" Stanley squealed, grabbing the mittened paws of his girlfriend and best friend and running to the door where they jumped upon Santa's sleigh in the cushioned seating, next to Santa Paws and Binky. It was a tight squeeze, but it was very snuggly.

"Adventure time!" Paddy hollered as they whooshed in to the sky.

Chapter 13

"Left!"

"Right!"

"Straight On!"

They yelled out instructions to a laughing Santa Paws as they were pulled through the skies by the two Sleigh-Dogs.

Mountains, lakes, seas, forests and rivers came in and out of view as they went.

But Stanley was disturbed suddenly as he looked down to a land full of rubble.

"What's that Santa Paws?" asked the curious dog, worried that it was going to be an answer he didn't want to hear.

"You really want to know?"

He nodded, as did his friends.

"It was once a beautiful country my dear friends but the humans, well, they destroyed it. They disagreed over lots of things and the argument got steadily worse over several years. Finally, they started to fight each other, and they went to war. Their country was destroyed, their people fled and no one won. That is all that remains".

"War? What is that good for?" Stanley asked.

"Absolutely nothing," Maisie replied, sadly.

"You can say that again," Paddy agreed.

Santa put his large, soft paw around all four of his small friends, thinking how sensible they were and glad the future was in their paws.

He decided it was time to head for home, the magic was running low and Embry would have a big mug of vanilla milk and gigantic slice of gingerbread house waiting for him. He turned the sleigh, ready to do a loop to cheer the youngsters up before they returned.

Something moved below and Stanley swivelled around, on to his knees, looking out over the back of the sleigh.

"Santa Paws Shay I just saw something move...look down there...a big grey dog," he screeched, waving his paws at a grey, cement patch beneath.

Binky, Maisie and Paddy turned around too and looked at where Stanley was pointing, but there was nothing.

"I think you are tired Stan, it's been a long day, there's nothing there," Binky asserted.

"No, I saw something, I did. I know I did. There's a big dog down there, abandoned. We need to rescue it and there's not a moment to lose," his eyes filled with tears, "there it is again!" he shouted, pointing over the shoulders of the others, who were all looking at him as he jumped up in his seat. "Paddy, Maisie...are we a rescue team or not?"

Santa Paws and Binky looked at each other and then at the three tzus with their pleading eyes.

"No harm in making sure," Santa Paws declared, "we'll fly down and do a quick investigation".

Chapter 14

They landed on a big grey hill and everywhere around them was landscaped in grey. It was cold, eerie, damp and amongst the rubble were bits of fence, coloured lights, signposts and bricks.

A deserted building was in front of them, with the word 'café' written on the outside but it was barely legible due to being covered in dust and grime.

There certainly wouldn't be any donuts served in that place today, so Paddy pulled his emergency bag of donuts from out of his coat's inside pocket. There were still about half left.

"I don't like it here," said a tearful Maisie. Stanley held her tight, knowing it was bringing back memories of the horrible place she was living when he had helped rescue her nearly two years ago.

There was no sign of the dog and Paddy wondered whether Stanley had imagined it. However, Stanley was sure.

"I know I saw something, I did. A massive dog, a grey one, with enormous ears".

Santa Paws reached down and picked up a piece of wood in the shape of an arrow, with words carved in to it.

'Reptile House & Spider Spectacular' he read to himself quietly, but Maisie had heard him.

"No, no, not spiders," she was terrified of them and started to sob in to Stanley's fur.

Paddy, as Chief Scout, took control.

"Ok, let's be quick. We need to look about in scout fashion to see if this dog is real. Stan, you look East with Maisie, Santa Paws you go North, I will go South and Binky, West. We will meet back here in five minutes, synchronise watches now".

"What?"

No one had moved, everyone was frozen to the spot, staring at him, wide-eyed with shock and pointing over his head.

"WHAT?"

Behind Paddy stood a large creature, helping itself to the donuts he held in his outstretched paw.

Stanley was right, he had seen a creature that needed rescuing.

But it was certainly not a dog.

Chapter 15

The baby elephant had been so pleased to see the little furs fly over her home. She had been so lonely and hungry since the people had taken her family and friends away leaving her behind that she had waved at the little white furry fella with the big eyes. She made him see her and she hoped he would drop by, because she could smell some food that smelt just like the aroma that used to come out of the café. She wondered if they would share like the children had before, when it was all happy.

When she was born here it had been a place full of laughter and smiling children but one day that stopped. Her parents hid her away in a cave with them and many of the animals did the same, seeking cover wherever they could. Some had run away and some, well, some just weren't around anymore.

She and her parents had each other and they wouldn't move from where they felt they were safe.

Then, a few days ago things changed, and she found herself alone. But now, it would seem, she had some new friends. She held out her trunk to them.

"Hi, I'm Vera, Vera the baby elephant". She pointed her hoof at a sign on the ground, with a picture of her and the words 'NEW ARRIVAL' written on it and a picture of her with her mum and dad.

Santa Paws stepped forward, he took her trunk in both his paws and shook it with warmth and affection.

"Hello Vera, an honour to meet you, I am Santa Paws Shay and these are my friends. We are dogs, of all shapes and sizes but still much smaller than you!"

He introduced them one at a time and they shook her trunk too. she giggled as their furry paws tickled her.

Santa Paws looked seriously at her and then at Binky, who shrugged at how this small girl was here alone as, of course, elephants were family animals.

"Vera, are you all alone here? How did that happen?" he asked as she nodded and began to tell her tale.

Chapter 16

This was such a happy place when I was a little baby. Mother, Father and I would have a lot of fun. We had people that cared for us and visitors every day as well as lots of other animal friends.

But then, the war began, everything changed, the people left and the animals too until, well, just a few of us remained. Even the spiders left.

I hoped that the good times would return but every day got a little sadder, with less to eat and quieter too. I don't like the quiet.

A few days ago, some lorries appeared, and my parents told me to hide real good and they tucked me away in our cave where I was to remain until they returned.

I heard voices, kind voices, and the people spoke of other elephants and a land of plenty many miles away. I heard them outside, but they said the little one must have perished and they needed to depart to safety in case of bad people and I stayed here like I was told.

But then I heard my father screaming "VERA VERA come out they are good people". He got louder and louder until I finally thought I should run out to see what good people were.

But I was too late. The lorries drove them all away and my father's voice got more and more distant and now, I am alone.

So, have you come to live here now doggies and will you be my friends?

"Of course, we will be your friends Vera, but not here. It's not safe for any of us. Dogs or elephants, we are in grave danger".

Shay looked concerned; he didn't know what to do.

But as he looked around, he realised he had the best rescue team with him. Tzus. More than used to rescuing those in peril.

It was time to hatch a plan. Quickly.

"I need to talk to my team Vera; you stay right there”.

He gathered his friends together in a huddle, there was no time to lose. They were in a warzone and it was dangerous.

Chapter 17

Shay was scared, he had excellent hearing and, in the distance, he could hear bad people and noises he didn't like the sound of. War noises.

"Tzus, we have to get us and, if possible, Vera out of here but there are many problems and I think it may be impossible to do it all now. There's a chance we might need to leave Vera behind and come back another time or arrange for a human rescue. She's too big to go on the sleigh. The humans were good, I saw it on the television at home with my lady, but they seem to have missed her. Maybe we can get them back to rescue her?"

The bad noises got louder; people were coming. They were in peril.

Paddy was in a panic, pacing around and wringing his paws.

"We can't leave her here now SP, can you hear the bad humans coming? They are just over that hill making scary noises. We all must go. Vera too".

"How much magic is left?" Maisie asked.

Shay opened the box. There was just enough to get home and a little spare.

"We can do it," Stanley decreed. "Remember last year when I took off when I ate the enchanted sprinkles?"

They nodded and, despite the seriousness of the situation, all giggled.

Stanley continued, undeterred.

"If we sprinkle some on Vera, then she will be able to fly, won't she? Well, then Paddy and I can ride on her back and follow the sleigh back to Santa Paws Palace and safety. Right?"

Binky wiped his brow and let out a long sigh.

"I don't know Stanley, we have never used it on any animal other than a dog and it might work, it might not, and it would be such a waste of good magic if it didn't work, you see the thing with magic is it takes a long time to cultivate and mature to the right strength to enable something to fly and the spell is only really at dog level and it hasn't been quality controlled for elephants, I think we might need a different licence for that and what if it doesn't work then we will be liable for any resulting damage or distress and..."

"Have you got another plan then?" Maisie interrupted, sharply, tapping her paw.

They could all hear the bad people, getting to the top of the hill near where the sleigh was parked with the Sleigh-Dogs waiting.

"No," Binky said, "Santa Paws?"

"Let's do this!" Santa Paws shouted.

He whistled and the Sleigh-Dogs started running towards them with a look of relief. He jumped on, pulling Binky and Maisie on too. He took a pawful of the Christmas Sprinkle Magic and flung it over the dogs so they started to hover.

"VERA YOU'RE COMING WITH US!"

Vera didn't hesitate. She ran over and Paddy and Stanley grabbed her ears and climbed on her back.

"We're gonna help you, we are going somewhere safe, paw promise!" Stanley told her.

"Don't be scared Vera, but it's time to see an elephant fly!" Paddy shouted.

Binky and Maisie threw pawful after pawful of magic over Vera and to everyone's delight she also began to hover.

She squealed with excitement as Binky stood up in his seat and flung the remains of the box in front of them to make an icy path for take-off.

WHOOOSH went the sleigh.

WHOOOOOOOOOSH went Vera, Paddy and Stanley.

Chapter 18

They were safe and free, flying through the night sky, past stars and clouds.

Vera was a natural flyer and Paddy and Stanley felt safe sat upon her.

Maisie and Binky were knelt on the sleigh seat facing backwards and feeding donuts to Vera as they went. She picked them out of their paws with her trunk, eating one and then passing one each to her riders in turn.

They laughed and smiled.

"A little turbulence as we descend, hold on to your elephant!" chortled Santa Paws.

Vera was thrown a little to the side as she followed the sleigh down towards the glistering palace turrets.

"Me hat!" cried Stanley, clutching his head.

"Me hat...and me muffs!" Paddy yelled, knowing he'd be in trouble with his Mam if he lost them.

"It's OK, I've got this!" Vera said. She swooped down, flying round in a circle and caught all three items on her trunk and plonked them back on to their heads.

Santa Paws was very happy. The trip hadn't turned out quite how he had expected but he had pushed himself out of his comfort zone, done something he had never done before and rescued an animal-less-fortunate. Even he, a dog of the world that knew so much, could learn something new.

'Maybe you can teach an old dog new tricks,' he thought as they came in to land.

Chapter 19

It was something of a surprise as Santa Paws, Binky, Maisie, Paddy and Stanley strolled in through the arched doors and in to the lounge with an elephant but, soon enough they were all gathered around and welcoming her.

Vera loved it. Everyone was introducing themselves, shaking her trunk and getting her drinks and snacks. She had a family once again – a loving, caring, hospitable dog family.

Embry took it in her stride quite calmly as they explained what had happened.

"Well, one thing is for certain, Vera can call Santa Paws Land home for this Christmas at least. We will make her at home in one of the outbuildings for now and work out what happens after that but, whatever happens, she will be loved and safe. Paw promise," she said, looking proudly at the team playing with their new elephant pal and making her chuckle.

"Not too many sweets for Vera please!" she instructed.

Santa Paws finally settled down with his warm milk and gingerbread in a comfy chair by the fire as the tzu team came to say goodbye.

"I'll just have this and then it's back to work for me," he said, "we will catch up on our schedule in a few days and I promise to try and pop in to see you all on Christmas Eve".

"Tzus of Tzu Kingdom you are amazing, you really are. An example to us all. This was meant to be, we were meant to find Vera and rescue her".

"As King Bailey says, 'It is as it was, as it is and as it always will be'. Safe journey home little ones – you are most definitely on the Nice List".

He smiled and relaxed in his chair as Embry stepped in and gathered them up in her paws.

"Time to get you little ones off home," she said, and they filed out of the lounge, tired but happy.

Stanley turned around as he left to check on Vera. She looked so at home that he decided it was best to tip-paw out and leave her to get cosy. She would be OK now.

They walked outside and Embry bark coded the door to the tunnel open and kissed them on their heads as she gave them all a box of gingerbread paws to take home to share.

But as Stanley stepped his paw into the tunnel he suddenly couldn't feel the ground under his paws any more.

"What the...I haven't had any magic sparkles...help!"

Paddy and Maisie laughed. Vera had lifted him up with her trunk, she had run after him to say goodbye.

"Stan, thank you for seeing me and saving me, thank you, you are indeed a wondrous little dog!"

"Oh Vera, I am just so glad you are safe and warm," Stanley said, wrapping his little paws around her, "and we're all one big team, right!"

His friends all smiled, it had been down to Stanley that Vera was safe, and it really was the true meaning of Christmas – Elephant or Dog it was a time for peace and love with friends and family.

From the desk of Santa Paws

The Palace of Santa Paws

Santa Paws Land

12th December 2017

King Bailey of Tzus

Tzu Kingdom

Via the Fairy Doors

My dear friend Bailey

Well, that turned out to be quite the adventure!

I wonder, are things ever quiet in Tzu Kingdom or when your little ones are around? LOL!

First of all, every one of the visitors behaved in an exemplary fashion. They were polite, thoughtful, kind and eager to learn. A credit to you and dear Queen Coffee as I have come to expect. I would not be surprised to see a few applications to join Team Christmas in the future.

Now, as you have no doubt heard, we rescued a young elephant called Vera who had been left behind in a zoo because of one of those pointless wars that the humans have. She was in mortal peril and, for a time, we were too. It is thanks to Stanley, Paddy and Maisie we rescued her – a few minutes more and it might have been a very different story.

It was incredibly humbling to watch your team organise a rescue with such bravery. In fact, I think Maisie was more worried about the spiders than staging an incredible rescue! Bailey, I am just Santa Paws and my job involves riding a sleigh, organising presents and spreading cheer but those three little shih tzus made me as brave as a lion and I am proud of what I, personally, achieved that evening under their guidance and with just a taste of their courage. I'm not necessarily in a hurry to do it again though Roh Roh Roh!

Vera now has a beautiful home in the outbuilding next to Santa Paws Palace and she has been helping us move and load the gifts for all the known dogs in the world. This got me to thinking and, after talking to Embry, we have offered her a permanent home and she has agreed.

We traced her parents, now settled in to an elephant park, safe from harm, and we got a message to them and a message back to little Vera but, the difficult thing is that you can't just drop a baby elephant in to a reserve as easily as you can drop a 'lost tzu' in to a garden in Swansea! She would never survive in the wild either.

She will, however, be a great asset to Santa Paws Land. You see, as you are aware, #TeamChristmas changes almost every year and a new Santa Paws will take over here when I retire, and it could be that important things are forgotten. But elephants never forget.

So, Vera has taken on the role of The Christmas Elephant and will live here, safe and loved, for as long as she wishes - hopefully for always - helping us create a wonderful Christmas for all the dogs of the world.

Well, King of Tzus, I wish you a wonderful festive time and I hope to drop in – not literally though – on Christmas Eve!

I hope you all enjoyed the gingerbread.

With a paw full of love to Coffee and you dear friend,

Shay

Tzu Kingdom

It's A Wonderful Kingdom

Chapter 1

"It's Christmas Eve Eve Morning!" shrieked Stanley as he jumped through his fairy door and landed in the Welcome Room.

Colin and Carmen giggled from the central desk. Indeed, it was and, with it, the culmination of his big Christmas project.

They laughed as he shimmied around the desk, wiggling his tail with jingle bell in each paw. Stanley Shih Tzu was certainly in the Christmas spirit as he sung…

Oh, you better not pout

You better not cry

You better not shout

Stan's telling you why

Santa Paws is coming to town

Shay's making his list

Binky's checking it twice

He's gonna confirm

That all dogs are nice

Santa Paws is coming to town

Santa Paws is comiiiiiinnnnnnnnnn to town

Chapter 2

Tonight, Santa Paws was coming to town, well, to Tzu Kingdom. Shay was to visit and have dinner with his dear friends King Bailey and Queen Coffee. They went back years and there was a special relationship between Santa Paws Land and Tzu Kingdom. There was also a happy photo of the three of them on Coffee's desk in the Royal Quarters.

Meanwhile, his trusted companion and chief elf-dog Binky, a Pekingese, would supervise the tzus loading the wonderful and thoughtful gifts on to the sleigh to be delivered across the world to all known dogs.

Stanley had also organised a spread in the café.

The tzus jumped as the door to Tzu Library shut loudly and King Bailey appeared, looking uncharacteristically shaken as he wandered through the Party Room.

By coincidence, Queen Coffee sashayed in to view, coming from the Comforter Wing, carrying a suit.

"Well, that told me!" said Bailey, smirking a little.

"What Bailey Boo, who told you what?" Coffee pondered, kissing her husband on his ear as he took her free paw in both of his.

"Well, I took my library books back and I went to climb up the rolling ladder to put them on their shelf only to be scolded by young Maisie! Apparently, I would just do it all wrong, so I was to leave them on her desk in a neat pile for her to attend to later and go about my kingly business!"

"Bailey was she insolent to you?" Coffee gasped.

Respect for elders was important to the Queen of Tzus and, although they had no furs and graces, she expected everyone to be respectful and polite to each other. Maisie was usually one of the most well behaved tzus, always so grateful that she had been rescued by Stanley, Paddy and Phoebe a few years ago from a terrible fate in a loveless home with a bad human lady.

"No, no, Coffee my love, not at all, she's just focused on her job and getting the library all shipshape so she can show Santa Paws Shay tonight. She's not stopped for days. No, not naughty at all, just focused on the job in paw...she reminds me of someone I knew when I was younger..." he sniggered, looking at Stanley, who knew exactly what he meant. Queen Coffee was Maisie's role model and there were more than a few similarities. Stanley wondered what Coffee was like when she was younger, when she was Chief Scout, or even before that when she was simply Miss Coffee. He thought she might have been a lot like Maisie.

Stanley was so proud of his girlfriend and wanted to share some news.

"Coffee, Bailey, do you know what Maisie will unveil in the library tonight for Santa Paws Shay?"

They both shook their heads.

"Well, she has pulled together all the Christmas books – books about the Santa Paws myths and legends, biographies and memoirs of all the Santa Paws there have been, maps and diagrams of Santa Paws Land, recipe books, picture books, toy catalogues, sleigh manuals...well, anything to do with Christmas for dogs. Some of the books are antiques, but they won't leave the library you see, she has put them under glass cases and if you want to look at them you have to open them on mini beanbags and wear white paw gloves to turn the pages".

The King and Queen smiled. Maisie was a lovely tzu with great leadership skills.

"Little Beth is helping too; she has to dust all the books and wear a special apron and fur net".

Beth was Maisie's little sister now. She had been rescued from a puppy farm by Stanley, Maisie and Paddy when Phoebe got trapped on a big rescue. With a little fairy magic, they had got them back to safety and, after time in the Comforter Wing, she was homed with Maisie and her new family.

"Well," said Queen Coffee, "I think this is going to be the best evening. I love Christmas Eve Eve...the anticipation of the fun ahead, spending time with friends and family, playing games, singing and dancing, wonderful food but also remembering those less fortunate than us and making sure they have a good time too".

A tear rolled down in to her beard and Bailey caught it on the reverse of his paw.

"It is a time for appreciating what we have and looking out for those that don't," he said.

"Oh Stan, you must be wondering what I'm doing with your best suit!" said the Queen. "Well, Maisie has insisted that you be in your best for when she takes Santa Paws Shay to the library. I had it cleaned for you, there were a few jam splodges and half a custard doughnut in the pocket, but it's all good as new now".

Stanley blushed, wondering how he had missed that half doughnut.

"Paddy said he would hang it in your locker in Scout Tower. He's due on his shift in a few minutes so I am meeting him here quickly".

Chapter 3

Right on cue, Paddy Chief Scout appeared behind them with his tall rescuer girlfriend Phoebe and burped. Loudly.

"Morning all!"

"Pads!!!" Stanley hugged his friend. "Have you just been through your fairy door, is that why you burped?"

Paddy grinned. "Erm, no, I think that was me pre-shift banana milkshake and pancake-maple-syrup-ice-cream-stack with side order of churros popping up to make your acquaintance!"

The boys screeched with laughter, Stanley holding on to Paddy whilst he chortled hysterically, gasping to catch his breath. Coffee and Phoebe rolled their eyes.

Coffee tapped her paw and waited for them to calm down.

Finally, she took Paddy's paws in hers and inspected them both sides.

"Hmmmm lemme see, no jam, no cheese, no gravy, no milkshake...all clean and dry," she passed him the clean suit. He giggled, he loved Coffee so much, he was her deputy until a couple of years ago, but he sometimes tried her patience! She loved him back, he had been her fast-tracked protégé and he wouldn't be Paddy without his crazy sense of humour, dramatic ways and healthy appetite!

"Hang Stanley's suit up, I'm trusting you with it mister. Quick like a bunny, we all have a busy day!"

Coffee looked wistful. The first time Stanley had worn his super smart suit King Wolfgang had been visiting, from another time, and a special luncheon had been held in his honour.

Wolfgang was the second ruler of Tzu Kingdom and went missing in a sea rescue in 1945, presumed lost for all time, but he wasn't. A time burp had thrown him forward and he reappeared in modern times. He had stayed with them for nearly a year, living in the bedchamber in the Royal Quarters and becoming so popular with everyone that they called him Wolfy, Uncle Wolfy to some of the youngest.

It had been wonderful to have him around and sad when he jumped back in the next time burp where he lived out the rest of his life, sending a message through time to let them know he had got back safely, even though he closed his eyes for the last time shortly after his return.

Coffee and Bailey often wondered if they would ever see him again, but the time burps were deemed unsafe and only to be used in desperate emergencies.

She clapped her paws, and everyone scarpered. Paddy climbed the rope ladder to Scout Tower clutching Stanley's attire, Phoebe skipped off to the Rescuer Den and Stanley pulled on his coat and boots and scampered out to the barn to check the toys.

Bailey took Coffee's paw, they smiled at Colin and Carmen on the welcome desk as they walked regally and elegantly to the café to thank the team for organising tonight's buffet and their own dinner with Santa Paws Shay.

Chapter 4

It was sunny yet chilly today and Stanley was glad of his good, sturdy grip boots. The ground was very muddy, slimy and slippery as he made towards the old barn. He had to slow down as he walked down the slope to the entrance where he had stored all the presents that had been donated fearing he would lose his balance.

He reached in his pocket for the key. Everything had been stored safe and secure on shelves, sorted by types, colours and size.

But, as he got nearer, he heard a sound he didn't like.

He could hear water dripping. He looked down at his paws by the barn door and they were sloshing in a puddle of dirty water. He gulped, fearing something terrible had occurred.

He unlocked the door but before he could turn the handle, a wave pushed the door open, knocking him to the ground. He squealed as he landed in a muddy puddle.

As he sat up, he peered in through to the barn. It was unrecognisable from what he had left yesterday.

He pulled himself up from the ground, his fur covered in gloopy mud and grime. He slowly entered the barn, hoping that everything was somehow going to be OK.

But as he surveyed the scene it was clear it was not. Every toy, every blanket and every snack lay floating in muddy water. Conscious that the building was brighter than before he looked up to see an enormous hole in the roof.

A rare storm in Tzu Kingdom had destroyed Christmas for the dogs-less-fortunate. There would be no presents this year and, Stanley reflected, it was totally his fault.

He had let Santa Paws down and Christmas was ruined.

Chapter 5

The little vanilla dog didn't think he would ever stop crying. His loving eyes were red and sore, the upset hurt in his tummy and pounded in his head.

He picked up teddy bear after teddy bear and they were full of yucky rain. He pulled out blankets and they were too waterlogged for him to even lift. The treats were all in pieces, no more than crumbs floating in dirty water.

He caught sight of himself in a window. His beautiful red and grey coat that Granny had bought him for being a good boy on holiday in York was filthy too and his boots were caked in mud.

He had to get away. He ran and ran until he couldn't run any more. Stanley fell to his knees and cried until his throat was sore. Looking around, he realised he didn't know where he was, but he thought this must be the very edge of Tzu Kingdom. There was a bridge over a river that must lead to another world. Still sobbing, he dragged himself over to it and held his head in his paws.

He was a failure - the worst. His tears ran down his beard and plopped in to the river. He couldn't ever imagine going back to Tzu Kingdom now. They would soon find out what he had done, and he wouldn't be welcome anyway.

Santa Paws would arrive tonight, and King Bailey and Queen Coffee would have to inform him that there were no presents for the dogs-less-fortunate this year. He would be polite of course and return to Santa Paws Land empty-pawed, striking Stanley off the good list and flying right past his house on Christmas Eve, not even delivering his gifts from his friends and family. 'That's OK,' he thought, 'they can go to some less fortunate dogs'.

The tears started to fall once again, and he looked in to the river.

A glow of light in the river startled him. It was magical. He wiped his tears. He could feel something behind him, and he swivelled around.

"Stanley, dear little friend, come here for a hug. Why the tears? Look at you, you seem to be in a most dreadful state. What can I do to help?"

A big, cuddly tzu sporting a majestic beard and a resplendent pair of dazzling angel wings stood before him. Stanley ran in to his outstretched paws.

"King Wolfgang!"

Chapter 6

Stanley sobbed in to Angel King Wolfgang's fur until he ran out of tears. They walked back in to the Kingdom a little and sat on a pretty bench by the Edelweiss patch.

Surveying Wolfgang, Stanley was mesmerised. He looked so healthy and fit despite being well, dead. He looked in the peak of glowing health and his wings illuminated his thick brindle fur. His eyes were bright and his plume as glorious as it had ever been.

"Wolfy, how did you get here? I mean, not to be rude or anything but aren't you, erm, I mean, didn't you…erm…well, I don't know how to say this..."

"Yes, Stan, I died, many years ago, after Bailey and Coffee got me back to my time. I was glad to return, even though I only got a few more weeks with Sally and Stella at least we were reunited, as a fur family. I see you got my message!"

"Now I am an angel, watching over you above the clouds with all the other fur angels. I am restored to my best beyond 'Biscuit Mountain'! Don't ask any more Stan, I cannot divulge further but, just to say, there's nothing to be afraid of up there…"

Stanley wanted to ask so much, but he honoured what Wolfgang said and kept his lips buttoned. The Angel King continued.

"So, today I was asked to return to the mortal world briefly, after seeing you in distress, to see what I could do to help. Please young man, explain what the problem is".

Chapter 7

With a heavy sigh, Stanley told the whole sorry scenario, right up to the part where he ran away and saw the glow.

"I can never go back Wolfy, never. I am a failure and a laughing stock. Maisie won't love me and, well, everyone will tolerate me of course but they will never feel the same about me and I don't suppose Maisie will even want to be seen with me anymore and that means I won't get to see Beth either because she won't want such a bad influence on her little sister and I love Beth as if she was my little sister too. I am so rubbish".

"Stanley, of course they still love you, everyone makes mistakes. Don't you think King Bailey or I ever got anything wrong?" King Wolfgang had never admitted it to his friends in the future, but it was his foolhardiness that got him trapped in a time burp in the first place. But he assumed that it was how it was meant to be. That was his excuse and he was sticking with it!

"You, Bailey, Coffee, Paddy, you always pull things around and it seems like they were meant to happen that way. Bailey always says 'it is as it is, as it was and as it always will be' so he knows, because he and Coffee are the chosen ones. I do silly things. I am nothing but a liability. No, it's best if I just jump back through my fairy door to Mama and Dad, put all notions and thoughts of Tzu Kingdom aside and just stop in the human world. Forever".

"Wolfy, I would be grateful if you could leave a note for me saying, 'goodbye from Stan, he loves you all, don't look for him, it's for the best. His doughnut stash is in his locker, under his spare uniform shorts'".

Purposefully, he got up and started to march back towards the main building.

"STANLEY SHIH TZU!" hollered Wolfgang, "you will break their hearts if you do that. Plus, I can't hold a pen now!" He pointed to his wings and shrugged.

The young tzu paused for a moment and hung his head.

"You're right, maybe I just have to put up with the consequences of my foolishness and just come through less and less until I'm just not important any more. Reduce my shifts in Scout Tower. Slowly wean them off me. You know Angel Wolfy, this is such a pickle. Maybe it would have been better if I had never discovered Tzu Kingdom at all".

Wolfgang stopped in his tracks and looked up to the sky. He nodded and winked.

"That could work," he whispered, still looking up.

"OK, Stanley, let's do this".

Wolfgang wrapped his paws and wings around Stanley, a bright glow enveloped them both and a chill wind whistled past. Stanley felt different and he didn't know why. He looked down. His boots were clean. He felt his coat and it was no longer covered in mud. He looked at his paws and his fur was bright and fluffy again.

"What just happened?"

Wolfgang smiled.

"You got your wish Stanley. You aren't here. You never have been. You never discovered Tzu Kingdom. Let us see what this world would be like without you".

Wolfgang grabbed Stanley around his middle, glowed and flew away with him in his grip.

Chapter 8

They landed somewhere horrible with a putrid smell.

Stanley looked around and he knew he had been here before. There was broken glass on the floor and a ramshackle kennel. He heard shouting and whimpering.

A big nasty lady with a bottle of beer and a cigarette was screaming at a little grey and white, matted tzu to get back in the stinky kennel.

A pain jolted through his body as he realised where he was and who was in the kennel.

"Wolfgang, this is the night of the day that I first came to Tzu Kingdom! I rescued my little Maisie, brave as a lion! Oh, you are going to get to see me being a hero – I went back for Maisie's teddy bear, Millicent, you know, the one in the Comforter Wing! She wouldn't leave without her and I even defied Phoebe to get her! How naughty of me, but I got them both safe. I tripped the bad lady up!" he laughed.

They watched together. Alice, Pom Pom, Phoebe and Paddy jumped through, followed by Franc.

"No, that's not right Wolfgang. I came through with Paddy. I volunteered…" his voice trailed off as he realised.

"You might have done Stanley, but now you haven't discovered Tzu Kingdom. You didn't meet Coffee, you don't know Paddy, you've never jumped through a fairy door and burped and you have never heard of the 'Paw Stomp'".

He watched on as Franc ran in to the kennel, just like he had done. Paddy interjected in their conversation just like the first time, Maisie sobbed, came out with Franc and jumped up to Paddy.

'Phew, it's all going to be ok, even without me,' he thought.

Half way back and the team were all running towards the fairy door and back to safety when Maisie started screaming for Millicent. Just like she did before, she wriggled out of Paddy's paws and ran back for her pink bear.

Stanley willed some fur to run after her like he had done, but the bad lady had appeared and, in this world, there was no fur to stop her. She chased them all as Maisie ran back to the kennel.

"It's not safe, it's not safe. Abort mission," Phoebe shouted. Obediently, they all jumped through to Tzu Kingdom leaving Maisie behind.

Stanley looked at Wolfgang for reassurance. "They go back for my Maisie, don't they?"

"Yes, the very next day," he nodded, "but she was nowhere to be seen, all that remained in the kennel was a teddy bear named Millicent. Maisie has not been seen since".

Chapter 9

A flash of light and they landed in another dank, grim environment. In the middle of a storm.

Stanley tried to figure out where Wolfgang had taken him this time. He could barely see through the driving rain and it was gloomy dark too. But then something happened; a fairy door opened, and he knew just where he was. It was the rescue of the twelve jewel and metal pups, their parents, Beth and her mother Molly.

It was the biggest rescue that had ever been attempted in Tzu Kingdom and the rescuers had been divided in to teams. There were twelve puppies and six adults to rescue, or so had been thought. When they arrived, they discovered two more – Molly and her puppy Beth, now Maisie's little sister. He remembered with fondness how Phoebe had fostered Beth after her mother had closed her eyes for the last time when they landed in the Welcome Room.

They watched the action unfold before them. It was a strange experience for Stanley. He had watched it all unfold once before from Scout Tower with Maisie, in awe at Coffee, still Chief Scout at the time, and Paddy in charge. The teams ran back and forth with puppies in their paws, helping the weak parent dogs run to safety. Then it happened, Phoebe heard a sound – which he knew now to be Molly shouting for help - and ran back in to the building only to be trapped with them.

"Wolfy watch this, Paddy, Maisie and me...we come through and rescue them. Watch, watch!"

Sure enough, Paddy jumped through the fairy door in his borrowed rescuer kit. But no one followed.

Stanley turned to Wolfgang, who shook his head sadly.

"You never discovered Tzu Kingdom Stan, remember, Maisie is who knows where. Paddy is all alone trying to rescue Phoebe".

Stanley wiped the tears from his eyes as he watched Paddy, panicked and frightened, try to open the door. Suddenly, a bolt of light hit the lock and the door flung open. It was the fairies! They were there helping just like the first time. Maybe it would be OK without him.

A little while later Paddy and Phoebe ran out with Molly and Beth, but it had taken longer than the first time. Blocking their way were three horrible, stinky, ugly men with bad teeth. They both watched in horror as they chased after them, Molly holding Beth tight.

It was no use, Molly was weak, and the men caught her, clinging to Beth.

"Save yourselves, run..." she cried with her last breath.

Paddy and Phoebe had no option, they ran back to Tzu Kingdom leaving dying Molly and her small puppy Beth behind.

Chapter 10

"I don't like this, I don't like this," cried Stanley, "I want to see something nice now..."

"Like Christmas?" suggested Wolfgang. To his little friend's nods, he covered him with his wings again and there they were, just at the moment when Santa Paws Shay crash landed in Tzu Kingdom.

Toys, gifts, teddies and treats bounced all around and the sleigh wheels buckled when it landed on top of Santa Paws, thankfully with him between the wheels and just banging his head slightly. Dogs of all shapes and sizes flew through the air in a terrifying display. How they all escaped serious injury Stanley would never know.

After a few minutes the doors flung open and Queen Coffee tore across the patio and to the sleigh where a motionless Santa Paws lay, calling his name.

Stanley watched and tried to think back to that night, even though it was a few years ago and he had forgotten some things. But, no, he was right. King Bailey ran to the sleigh too.

He turned to Wolfgang to ask but thought better of it. Without his presence in Tzu Kingdom Maisie and Beth were unaccounted for at present and he didn't want to think about any more bad things. Anyway, this was the year that Bailey delivered the gifts, maybe he was getting changed in to his Santa Bailey suit.

The scene dissolved away as Santa Paws and Team Christmas were carried and helped in to the Comforter Wing but there was still no sign of Bailey and they found themselves inside as Coffee, Mabel and Myrtle tended to the wounded. Stranger still, Coffee was in a scout uniform and not wearing the stunning green dress that had made her husband go "hubba".

'Paddy will be in shortly with his brother Mitch to fix the sleigh,' he thought. But Paddy never arrived, and the scene dissolved away once more.

Now, a party of dogs from Santa Paws Land had arrived and were talking with the Queen. They picked up Santa Paws on a stretcher and loaded him on to a plain, wooden sleigh, sprinkled some Christmas sprinkles and flew away above the clouds. They returned minutes later, taking the team in stages and flying them home.

"It's really only good for firewood now," said a small terrier called Pixie, looking over the Christmas sleigh as they took the final casualties away.

She went over to Coffee to comfort her.

"Shay will be fine in a few days and we can build a new sleigh for next year. Team Christmas will ride again sweet Coffee – it's only one Christmas and, well, we didn't have anything for the dogs-less-fortunate anyway. No, no tears, these things happen".

"Look, let me talk to Embry, maybe you can come and spend a few days with us, bring Bailey too and he can talk with Shay whilst we have a Pamper Night. It will do you both the world of good. We have to get Bailey back to his old self…things can't go on like this much longer, something will have to change, look at you my darling girl, your eyes are heavy, your ears are flat and there's nothing of you...it's making you ill with worry".

Stanley looked at Wolfgang, he didn't know what was going on and he needed some straight answers.

"Wolfy, please, it didn't happen like this, it doesn't make sense. We delivered the presents and we went to Hotel Battenberg in Paris to see Louis the Canine Concierge and we flew over the River Seine and we ate snails, well spat them out, and Bailey was Santa Paws for the night and Coffee was so proud of him. I need to talk to my best friend, I want to see Paddy, back in today time".

Wolfgang was melancholy too; he loved Coffee and Bailey after spending such a long time with them and this was difficult to watch, but there was worse to come.

Chapter 11

As the glow from his angel wings cleared, Wolfgang looked at Stanley with a face full of concern. This was going to be tough.

Stanley looked around to see where he had been taken this time. He was back in the Welcome Room. It looked familiar but not as clean, plush and fragrant as usual. The desk was unusually empty with a neat paw-written note that said, 'back later x'.

"Where is he? Where's my BFF Paddy? Is he in Scout Tower?" he asked enthusiastically. Wolfgang nodded towards the café and Stanley scampered in.

He looked on their normal table and stood on a chair for a better view. At the uncharacteristically quiet bar was a tzu that looked like Paddy, just thinner, with deep sad eyes and slumped shoulders. He would order a milkshake and ask the bartender.

As he waited for his shake he looked again at the sad chap and got a shock. It was Paddy, but not the cheery chap he knew and loved.

"Paddy?" he ventured, still not totally sure.

"What?" said a gruff bark.

"It's me...Stan...your best friend...for...forever..."

He looked Stanley up and down.

"I don't know you, never seen you before in me life. Plus, I don't have friends. Well, not anymore".

Stanley noticed something else about his bestie's appearance.

"Paddy, why are you not in your scout uniform?"

He rolled his eyes and sighed as he answered.

"Why would I be? I gave that caper up long ago, thankless task. Pointless too".

"No, no, you rescued loads of tzus-less-fortunate and brought them to safety..."

"Maybe a few, but not enough to make it worth all that peering through telescopes and climbing up ropes".

"No, no Paddy you're Chief Scout, everyone loves you and looks up to you and you're my hero...".

"Look 'snowflake fluffy chops', I don't know who you are or where you dropped in from, but I just like to be left alone here with my thoughts, thank you very much. I haven't been up that rope since my action girl Phoebe and I tried to rescue every fur from that puppy farm, and we lost two. The girl of my dreams has never been to Tzu Kingdom since so I'm just not interested, and I only come here every day just so I can be here to apologise for ruining her life if she happens by and once that's done then I'm never coming back either".

Stanley staggered and grabbed on to the bar rail.

"But Paddy, what about Queen Coffee and King Bailey? Our friends? They're the chosen ones remember?"

"Pfft, what? Ha de har har! OK, I can believe that of Coffee but that Bailey? 'Chosen-to-stay-in-his-office-whilst-poor-Coffee-runs-herself-ragged-one' more like".

"Coffee is Chief Scout, she helps out in the Comforter Wing because Franc is still traumatised from the rescue that went wrong because of that teddy bear, she tries to keep the Welcomer Room going, she's constantly trying to get furs to organise events they don't want to go to any more and then she's got to run around being ruler because King Bailey is ill...or so it's rumoured. We barely see fluff nor fur of him since that rescue... Santa Paws crashed here a couple of years ago and he didn't even come out then, he left Coffee to it and then refused an invitation to take the Queen on holiday to see the ice palace and - my dog - she needs a break. The Kingdom is crumbling away and it's never going to be rebuilt..."

Stanley couldn't take any more, he ran and ran back to the Edelweiss patch with Wolfgang flying behind him, his wings flapping faster and faster as he gathered pace.

He flung himself on the floor but there was no Edelweiss. Wolfgang flopped to his knees next to him and held him tight.

"Where's your flower patch, it's where you're buried and we tend it in your honour and now it's gone," he sobbed.

"I didn't make it back either Stan, not in a world where you were not," he explained, to more tears.

"Oh Wolfgang, what about Vera? My elephant friend? If Santa Bailey never happened then Shay never invited us to Santa Paws Land and maybe we never found her".

Wolfgang held him again, "I'm sorry, you never were there and you, Paddy and Maisie never went on a flight with Santa Paws and Binky. Vera got taken by the bad men".

"'Believe in the Kingdom' King Bailey used to say when everything was good. 'It's bigger than all of us' he said, and I did believe, I do believe...I...I..."

"Stan, Stan, to believe in the Kingdom it means you have to believe in yourself first and you did, and you should. Every dog's life touches so many others that you must never doubt the part you play in the world. The day you discovered Tzu Kingdom, followed Coffee's instructions and then took Paddy's paw and jumped through your fairy door with a burp, well, it started a chain reaction and you touched lives and events unfolded. In your own ways, each and every one of you is a chosen one and it ***is*** as it is, as it was and as it always will be".

Stanley sobbed uncontrollably in to his paws. "I want to discover Tzu Kingdom again. I want to discover my magical place and all my friends."..

Through his fur he saw the angel glow again and he dreaded to think where he would be now, it just couldn't get any worse.

"Stan! There you are pal, I've been looking everywhere for you, I am exhausted, we've all been so worried. We saw what happened and I ran down, I've been looking for you since. Everything will be fine now we know you're safe. Coffee and Bailey told Mac, Phoebe and me to keep on looking until we found you and Maisie and Beth went up Scout Tower to look through the telescopes with Winny and Bonz. What? Why you staring at me? What? Have I dropped gravy on me uniform shirt again...or jam?"

"Paddy, oh Paddy!" he squealed jumping up and hugging his pal.

Chapter 12

The Edelweiss patch had returned, Paddy was in his paws and he was all muddy again. His bad dream was over. Stanley sat on the bench and told his best friend everything that had happened since he ran away.

Paddy laughed and checked his pal's head for bruises.

"You must have had a boing on the bonce when you fell over by the barn," he laughed, "let's get you checked over in the Comforter Wing. Franc and Centime are on shift oh, with Otto too!"

Stanley smiled at the mention of Franc on duty.

"Maybe," he replied, "but it seemed so real when King Wolfgang, Angel King Wolfgang I mean, hugged me. His fur was soft and warm just like when he lived with us and his wings were, well, sparkly and magnificent".

Paddy nodded. If that's what his best friend believed, he would go with it. But he explained to his friend, maybe they should just keep it to themselves, a special secret to share and Stanley agreed. Maybe it was just a dream and something that he needed to figure out. Paddy had agreed though, there was certainly truth in what Wolfgang had said about believing in yourself.

"I wonder what Tzu Kingdom would be like if you hadn't discovered it Pads," Stanley mused.

"There'd be many more doughnuts to eat Stan!" They laughed, just like they had earlier when Paddy did his big breakfast burp.

The boys stood up and held each other tight. Paddy poked him in the ribs and made him giggle.

"Come on, me muddy fluffy chops bestie, let me show you what's happened whilst you've been hanging around in the clouds..."

Chapter 13

"Look who I found..." Paddy announced, proudly, as he led Stanley through the patio doors to the Royal Chamber.

"Oh, thank dog," exhaled Coffee as she collapsed in to her beanbag and started sniffing, "I have been worried sick, I haven't stopped wringing my paws".

"Stanley, Stanley, where have you been?" King Bailey cried as he saw his little friend come in to the room. He went to hug him, but saw him covered in mud, thought better of it, and held out his paw to shake.

"He's alright now KB, QC. He got a little overwhelmed when he saw the barn and he thought everything was ruined and it was all his fault. He even thought we wouldn't love him or want him in Tzu Kingdom any more..."

"Why...why would he even think that let alone say it?" Queen Coffee gasped, blowing her nose with her embroidered handkerchief, tearfully taking a sip of water and dropping her hanky in to a small laundry bin as she paced around the office. She checked Stanley over herself and rubbed a sore spot on his head, telling him just to be alert in case he felt at all dizzy or started to hallucinate.

Paddy chuckled in to a cushion, thinking of Stanley's angel dream.

Bailey had something to tell him, but he had to get him tidied up for the evening.

"Well, I think there's something you need to see but first a shower, I think! Stanley, why don't you use my bathroom here and make yourself handsome for tonight. I'll ask Mac to bring your suit down and I think we should be able to get your lovely new coat and boots clean before you go home," he winked at his wife.

Paddy raised his eyebrows. Wow, Stanley must be highly thought of if Bailey was going to let him use his own royal bathroom and shampoos but, he supposed, he could see he had been through a terrible ordeal and, as always, the King knew just what to do.

Chapter 14

Stanley smelt divine and felt amazing in his suit. Coffee had tied one of her patterned scarves around his eyes and they had walked him through to the Party Room.

As he got closer, smiling from ear to ear, he could smell soap suds but didn't know if it was his fur as it hit the corridor air or something else. Maybe it was just his coat being washed.

"He's here, he's back!" Phoebe shouted as he arrived, and she whipped off his blindfold.

"TA DA!" yelled Maisie, atop a table in the middle of the room. "Welcome to the Christmas Eve Eve laundry!!!!"

She jumped off the table and ran to Stanley, "hello my gorgeous boyfriend, let me show you around".

Maisie explained what had occurred whilst Stanley was running away.

The scouts saw what happened just after and ran down to the barn, they called Bailey and Coffee and they went to assess the situation with Mac, Kiki and Lola. They picked up the teddy bears, squeezed and prodded them and realised that if they moved quickly they could have them washed, hung out to dry, brushed and as good as new by the time 'Team Christmas' arrived. It was the same with the blankets and cushions.

The treats were ruined, but Mac had a plan for that. He ran to Tzu Bakery and spoke to Jiro, Acting Head Baker, who called in his top team to bake trays of wholesome treats. By tonight, they would be gift boxed with ribbons and ready to go.

Together, as a team, they wheeled out the incident board and hatched a plan.

The bears and blankets needed to be moved down to the main building and piled up outside the Party Room where the laundry would be based. Kiki and Lola called for help and a shih-tzu-chain was formed. They picked up a bear at a time and passed it along hundreds of pairs of paws through the Kingdom grounds and back in to the building. A relay of wheelbarrows moved the heavy blankets in the same direction.

Back at the laundry dozens of buckets had been filled with soapy water, tarpaulin had been laid across the floor and clothes lines had been fixed from one side of the hall to the other.

They divided in to four teams and they would rotate, taking an allocation of gifts to wash, dry, hang and brush.

Alice & Pom Pom, Brickie & Hiro, Sammy & Percy and Louis & Colin would lead a team each with Phoebe and Maisie in overall charge.

The dry blankets were being folded and the dry bears would be redressed with neat bows and ribbons from Coffee's haberdashery cupboard. Everything was loaded into the boxes Santa Paws Land Palace Manager Embry had sent through a few days ago, now with the contents listed neatly on the outside.

In the gift wrap department, paws were a flurry! Beth had drafted in her friends Bella and Millie to tie bows and brush teddy bear fur.

Scout Winny had joined Bentz in the café and they were ferrying in drinks and refreshments to order.

It was amazing to watch. The last lot were just going in wash buckets now.

Paddy hugged his pal.

"We're a team here in Tzu Kingdom Stan, never forget that! Believe in the Kingdom right?"

"...and believe in yourself too Paddy," he smiled.

Chapter 15

That evening, King Bailey straightened his new tie that his wife had left on his desk. It was extremely smart – silver and mulberry stripes that coordinated beautifully with his anchor grey suit. He buttoned his waistcoat and admired himself in the mirror. Waistcoats had become very popular this year after the Football World Cup and he felt rather dashing and distinguished, as well as terribly trendy despite his advancing years.

"Well, will I pass?" woofed a voice and he turned to see Queen Coffee - elegant in a long dress with batwing sleeves, mulberry to match his tie, with a silver crocheted shawl around her shoulders.

"HUBBA!"

"Silly Bailey," she giggled as she approached him, feeling assured that she had her look just right. She straightened up his tie to her liking and unfastened his bottom waistcoat button.

"Always leave the lowest one undone Bailey, there...King Handsome!" she smiled.

Paw in paw, they walked to their patio doors for the imminent arrival of Santa Paws and to where a magical spectacle greeted them.

In addition to the white lights that lit up the orchard and twinkled in the night sky, hundreds of tzus with colourful flashlights stood in line to light his path and welcome him to Tzu Kingdom. They eagerly anticipated his arrival and looked to the stars but, up in Scout Tower, Winny had the best view on the special ops telescope and, as soon as he was seen Mac, leaning out of the Scout Tower window with a megaphone, would alert them.

Scout Tower was illuminated too, and it was Stanley who saw both scouts jumping up and down. He laughed and prodded Maisie as Mac hollered to them.

"SANTA PAWS IS IN TOWN! E.T.A. ONE MINUTE!"

The shih tzus shuffled in to an orderly line and shone their torches on the ground to make a rainbow path. Santa Paws' sleigh came in to view as a little red dot in the night sky, after a few seconds they could see the six dogs pulling the sleigh and finally it swept to a halt in front of them. They all cheered and waved but something was not quite as expected. It wasn't Binky the elf sat next to him, but Pixie, his despatch manager.

"Where could Binky be?" Maisie asked Stan, with a furrowed brow.

Chapter 16

Santa Paws stood up and waved at the cheering crowds. He jumped on his seat and appealed for quiet.

"Has something happened to Binky?" Stanley asked Bailey, who shrugged.

"Furs, friends, Tzu Kingdom...thank you for inviting me along tonight on Christmas Eve Eve and I look forward to my tour and scrumptious dinner with your rulers, my friends King Bailey and the beautiful Queen Coffee. Last time I was here I think I was a little dizzy!"

Every fur laughed.

"Now, I would like to introduce Mrs Pixie Dust my despatch manager at Santa Paws Land who has come with me to help you all with loading and arrives bearing gifts of gingerbread, fur clips and bow ties for you all!"

"Santa Paws, where's Binky?" interrupted a concerned Paddy, stopping the cheering from the crowd.

"I was just coming to that Paddy my friend; Binky is on his way on an alternative mode of transport. If you look to the skies again, they should be arriving any..."

A squeal came from Scout Tower and an announcement was made on the loud speaker.

"THERE'S AN ELEPHANT APPROACHING TZU KINGDOM!"

"VERA!" yelled Stanley, Maisie and Paddy.

Chapter 17

Vera had grown since the tzus had last seen her, she wouldn't be fully grown until she was 15 but still, she was big compared to them and everyone laughed and cheered as she picked up her little friends in her trunk and raised them above her head!

Maisie, Paddy and Stanley screamed playfully as she bounced them up and down.

"I'm gonna be sick..." shouted Paddy.

"Untrunk us Vera..." laughed Maisie, waving to Beth on the ground, desperate to be picked up by an elephant trunk like her big sister.

She placed the three of them carefully on the floor and Stanley hugged her tight around her knee.

"I can't believe you're actually here," he said, stepping back and looking in to her eyes. Maybe the whole Angel King Wolfgang thing had been a daydream, but he knew, in his heart, that it really was down to him – and him alone – that Vera was rescued last year. He had spotted her and convinced Santa Paws to set down and look for the grey creature he saw in the war-torn abandoned zoo. Without him, she would have been captured by the bad men they had heard.

"Stan, Stan," Vera hugged him back, sensing he was upset, "I love it at Santa Paws Land. Embry looks after me as if I was her own puppyphant and I get fabulous food. My little outbuilding is so warm and cosy and...I have a job! I am the Christmas Elephant and I help Pixie and every fur with lifting and packing. That's why I am here today, I am going to help you load the presents on to the sleigh!"

"Oh Vera, I am so proud! Well, the gifts are all stacked up in the Party Room. We should get to work! I have done a spread and there are jam sandwiches and iced buns – you'll like them!"

Maisie coughed to get everyone's attention.

"Come on pals. The sooner we get packing, the sooner we can all enjoy the spread and I have to show Santa Paws around Tzu Library first!"

She skipped inside and everyone followed.

Coffee looked on, little Maisie was amazing.

"See you in a bit Santa Paws Shay. Enjoy your private dinner," Binky said as he followed the tzus to collect the presents.

"Oh, Binky, I forgot to brief you on something..." Shay yelled, running after him.

Pixie turned to the royal couple, she had just been to the sleigh and returned wheeling a crate of pretty gifts decorated with ribbons.

"These are from Embry from every fur at Santa Paws Land, plenty of fun things to share".

"Now, you two must visit in the spring. Shay's time as Santa is coming to its natural end and he so wants to entertain you two before he retires and becomes 'Santa Paws Emeritus'. He's asked Embry to redecorate the guest wing for you and it's going to look gorgeous. He wants to show you around the ice palace and show you all he's done, then he said, ice skating, s'mores on his balcony and a flight!"

Coffee looked at Bailey. She didn't ask, but her eyes lowered. Santa Paws Land was a winter wonderland and, being Canadian, she loved the snow and so wanted to see the incredible ice palace but there was always so much to do in Tzu Kingdom. Bailey knew just what to do, once again.

"We would love to come Pixie, please tell Shay and Embry to book us in for the first weekend in April!"

Coffee squealed and kissed her husband, then hugged Pixie excitedly.

Santa Paws Shay re-joined them to the news that he would soon have visitors.

"Oh, how marvellous. Roh Roh Roh, we had better get some heated blankets and warm mittens in for you King B, you're not one for the cold!" he laughed. He really wasn't! Coffee was perfectly at home running through snow, he preferred to watch a winter wonderland from inside, or on the TV.

"Well, I think it's dinner time, via Tzu Library," Coffee announced. Pixie scampered off to help with the presents and the three rulers of two important dog worlds went to enjoy a sublime dinner - not as heads of state, but as friends, paws reaching across lands, all working and striving for a better world.

Chapter 18

Shay flopped in to a pile of beanbags and laid his paws on his tummy.

"Well, that's me set up for tomorrow evening!" he chortled in his gruff, deep bark.

"You can't beat a Tzu Kingdom dinner," said Bailey as he passed him a tumbler of his aged malt, "how was the Christmas pudding? It's been maturing for months!"

"Delicious," Shay informed his old friends, "and thank you for the tour. The library, especially the Christmas section, and the gallery are amazing, Scout Tower is a triumph and I have never felt such warmth as I felt in the Comforter Wing. You say no one but a rescuer ever gets in to the Rescuer Den?"

"Nope," replied Bailey, and I concluded even before I was King that it was probably best left that way. Goodness knows Coffee had tried to get in many times over the years!"

Coffee sniggered, sipped her vodkatini and then pricked up her ears, to everyone's delight. "Can I hear singing? The piano?"

She could. In the party room the presents were all stacked on the sleigh and the spread was being consumed whilst Brickie played Christmas music so his friends could enjoy a sing song.

"Oh, Shay, Bailey, let's go and join in!"

Queen Coffee loved to sing and had a stunning choral bark. They ran after her and watched lovingly as she ran to join everyone at the piano. Vera was watching from the patio, her trunk through the doors, an elephant almost in the room and, by the enormous tree Stanley, with Beth in his paws (happy after a trunk lift from Vera), and Maisie were thanking everyone for their help.

"Jingle bells, jingle bells
Jingle all the way
Oh what fun it is to ride
In a six-dog open sleigh

Dashing through the snow
In a six-dog open sleigh
Through the stars we go
Laughing all the way.

HO HO HO

Bells on tzu-tail ring
Making spirits bright
What fun it is to ride and sing
A sleighing song tonight.

OH Jingle bells, jingle bells
Jingle all the way
Oh what fun it is to ride
In a six-dog open sleigh".

They gasped as Coffee joined them in the last chorus and began to sing.

Mac passed her the roving mike and winked at Brickie, they knew she would arrive and want to sing along. Shay lifted her up on to the piano and she began her favourite Christmas number.

"Sleigh dogs sing, are you listening?

On scout tower, snow is glistening

A beautiful sight

We're happy tonight

Walking in Tzu Kingdom Wonderland

Gone away is the bluebird

Here to stay is a new bird

He sings a love song

As we go along

Walking in Tzu Kingdom Wonderland

After cake, we'll conspire

As we snuggle by the fire

To face unafraid

Rescue plans that we've made

Walking in Tzu Kingdom Wonderland

When it snows, Coffee loves it

Bailey watches, wrapped in blankets

Furs frolic and play, the Team Christmas way

Walking in Tzu Kingdom wonderland".

Chapter 19

After a lovely evening, it was time for Team Christmas to depart.

They all said their goodbyes, with tummies full of a little too much delicious, festive food and drink. As they stepped outside, it had just started to snow, and it sparkled brightly as their paw prints appeared all around.

Vera stroked her little friends with her trunk. It had been good for them to be together again for the evening and it had been a lovely surprise too.

Stanley saved his hug until last and he giggled when Vera picked him up again. She held him close and whispered in his ear.

"Stan well, I wonder if you would give something some thought?"

He nodded.

"Thing is, Santa Paws Shay is going to retire soon and, well, I am an elephant as you know and I could live 50, 60 years or more and, during my time, I will serve many a Santa Paws".

Stanley nodded again; he was sad about this but he knew the day would come. It was hard work being Santa and ten years was enough. Shay deserved a happy retirement too as he reached his golden years.

"It's just, maybe you could be Santa Paws next? You would be perfect and you have the experience and, well, I would love to be your puppyphant!"

"No, me? I am so little, I couldn't be big and commanding like Shay and I don't have the skills!"

"Smaller dogs than you have been Santa Paws and well, Shay would teach you all you needed to know. Just say you'll think about it?"

Stanley laughed. "OK, of course I will Vera my friend! Love you to the moon!"

He landed back on the floor and Vera picked up Pixie who was flying home with her. They waved as they ascended in to the stars and back to the palace.

Binky high pawed his friends, promising to pop by soon and jumped up to the sleigh ready for Santa Paws.

The royal party came out on to the patio.

"We will see you in the spring Shay, please be careful tomorrow night and spread love throughout the world as you always do".

"I will King B and I hope that the world will be more fur and more like Tzu Kingdom one day".

He kissed Coffee's paw.

"Take care of this lovely lady King B, Santa's always watching!" He winked.

They laughed, shook paws and waved as Santa Paws Shay walked happily to his sleigh, with tzus clapping as he went. He stopped briefly to hug Paddy, Maisie and Stanley and then, with a little sprinkle of Christmas magic, he was gone.

Chapter 20

Stanley changed back in to his clean fresh coat and pulled on his boots.

He wished Paddy and Phoebe a Merry Christmas. They would all be back tomorrow for the Christmas Eve party and by Christmas Day they would be ready for a good long snooze! Paddy would be extremely tired as, like every Christmas since he had his family, he would spend the night by the oven, watching the turkey cook, barely blinking.

Stanley took Maisie back to her fairy door and watched as she ran down the garden to join Beth who had been taken home to bed by Mac some time ago before she got tired and tearful, she was still just a pup.

He hurried back through Maisie's door, through the corridor in to and immediately out of the Welcome Room and back in to his garden. He burped loudly and when the noise stopped echoing, he heard Mama calling him.

"Stanley...Stanners...there you are darling; you're fascinated with that old tree!"

He jumped up in to her arms and kissed her face. He loved her so much.

"Come on darling, we have to get going, Granny is expecting us, Dad's just loaded up the car. There's pie at Granny's house!"

Stanley felt a bit green; he didn't think he could possibly eat another thing but he would try.

They climbed up the steps together and Stanley paused to look up at Edinburgh Castle. Dad stepped through the patio doors and he picked him up and kissed him, with another kiss from Mama following swiftly. He loved his home as much as he loved Tzu Kingdom. His daydream about King Wolfgang visiting him as an angel had made him appreciate everything he had, and he smiled a happy smile. For a second, he wondered how Mama, Dad and Granny would cope without him. What would they even have to talk about? He shuddered, there had been enough of those types of thoughts today. He wasn't going anywhere.

'It's a wonderful life,' he sighed, with a happy head.

Mama smiled back and then looked curiously at his coat.

"What's this in your pocket Stan? Wow, what sort of bird did this come off? It's huge and it sparkles in the light, look, it's so pretty".

She added it to the Christmas plant arrangement on their dining table as they locked up and headed off for Christmas at Granny's.

But that feather wasn't from a bird and Stanley knew it. It was a wing feather from an Angel King. He looked to the sky and woofed.

"Happy Christmas Wolfy".

Authors' Note

Originally, 'Santa Bailey' was written as a promotional story to promote the Tzu Kingdom book series. But, as is often the case, the magic took hold.

There was a conundrum though.

We wanted Stanley to be in the book so it couldn't take place before Book One and so it needed to be a story that worked on its own. We also wanted Bailey (Karen's shih tzu) to be in the title just as Stanley (Gill's shih tzu) was in the title of 'Stanley's Discovery'. Looking to popular culture as we often do, the Christmas song 'Santa Baby' popped in to our heads and we had a title!

We needed to cast a Santa Paws and we knew this couldn't be a shih tzu, it had to be bigger than just this world. We also felt that this was time to tell readers that there were many magical dog worlds, one completely dedicated to Christmas magic. We looked at the many friends our boys had made on twitter and there we saw him. Generous of spirit, cuddly, kind and loving – Seamus the soft coated wheaten terrier from the USA. This is his story – a wonderful Santa Paws who believes that Christmas magic sparkles all year round with his Team Christmas!

It also meant we could cast some other dogs that weren't shih tzus and readers would, we hope, enjoy meeting many different dogs in the Santa Paws stories, especially when we visit Santa Paws Land.

After Book One was published, we started to think about another Christmas story. We had both been affected by stories of abandoned zoos in war torn countries and from this, we created our baby elephant character, Vera. Once we created her, we had to rescue her and so we looked to Santa

Paws Shay once again to make it possible. With the assistance of Stanley, Paddy and Maisie he did not disappoint!

The real Bailey's rescue was something that Karen had always wanted to be in a book. He is named after George Bailey from the film 'It's A Wonderful Life' and this was our inspiration. For a long time, we tried to work out how to put Bailey or Coffee at the centre of this story, but it just didn't work. In the original film, the point is that George Bailey is just a regular guy who didn't realise he had touched people's lives. That could not work with royalty.

Then one day an epiphany. What if Stanley had never discovered Tzu Kingdom? The more we unpicked this, the more we realised it would be catastrophic. Maisie, Beth and Vera would never have been rescued and it would have a disastrous effect on Bailey, Coffee, Phoebe and Paddy. By now, we had also created a much-loved angel and could cast King Wolfgang in the 'Clarence' role. It broke our hearts to create – even briefly – a dystopian version of Tzu Kingdom but we had to do it. Our own delight when Stan 'wanted to discover again' just like George Bailey 'wanting to live again' was evident!

It was perfect and, once again, we see every fur working together to save Christmas.

We love our Christmas stories and so, supported by Shay and his Lady, we have brought them all together in a special souvenir book for you to treasure.

Just one more thing...children of 1971 Gill and Karen grew up in the UK in the 1970s/80s and there was one staple on TV at Christmas way back then, when there was no Internet and only three channels - Morecambe and Wise! They discovered a shared love of those innocent days and, particularly, the song 'Bring Me Sunshine'.

So, here are their little sunbeams, as Eric and Ern...

Bailey & Stan

Bringing us sunshine...

TZU KINGDOM WORLD

Visit www.tzukingdom.com

for information on all our books, release updates and news.

Find 'Tzu Kingdom' on Facebook, Twitter and Instagram

See www.toonpetz.com to have your pet illustrated in the Tzu Kingdom style.

Karen Chilvers was born in Essex in 1971 and lives in Brentwood with King Bailey and his cat brother Dillon with Louis Battenberg as a regular visitor. She much prefers Tzu Kingdom to the real world and has a fairy themed garden.

Gill Eastgate was born in Edinburgh in 1971. As a child she wanted a pony but ended up with a rabbit. Stanley is her first dog who has, quite simply, changed her life. She lives in a suburb of Edinburgh with Stan and her husband Ray, who is affectionately known as 'The Tzu Father' due to his tzu-inspired beard.

Karen and Gill met in 2013 through Bailey and Stan after they both joined Twitter and introduced their mums to each other, knowing they had a lot in common. They first met in person in 2015, when Karen rocked up to Edinburgh for the festival and ensconced herself in Gill's house for three days. Stan slept on her bed and it was during that trip that the first part of the Tzu Kingdom series was scribed.

Many of the dogs in Tzu Kingdom are based on real dogs throughout the world that met on twitter forming firm and lasting friendships.

Acknowledgements

Karen would like to thank her mum for being there always, her sister Claire for giving her someone to have a wild imagination for in her youth, her nephew Freddie for allowing her to bring that back to life but, most of all Bailey, her inspiration.

Gill would like to thank the wonderful world of Twitter, after all, without it Karen and Gill would never have met. Her mum just for being her mum, her husband Ray for listening intently to the happenings in Tzu Kingdom without thinking she was completely mad, her wonderful Shih Tzu Stanley and, of course, her much loved and sadly missed Dad.

Karen and Gill both wish to thank actor Callum Hughes for voicing Stanley in the short film 'Stanley's Secret', Michelle Smith and ToonPetz.com for the beautiful illustrations that have also raised funds for furs-less-fortunate, Wendy Simko for designing this book's special cover and all their fur-friends across the world that have equipped a bus, supported us and made us laugh and cry over the years.

We love you to the moon.

Lightning Source UK Ltd.
Milton Keynes UK
UKHW010618141019
351570UK00001B/186/P